Pride Festival

by

NICOLE PYLAND

Pride Festival

When Ruby Simon wanted something, she usually got it and didn't mind working hard for it. Her small town had never done anything for Pride month, and she was determined to change that. Starting with a parade would be a little much, so Ruby started planning a festival.

Chance Curtis was used to always being pulled into her best friend's orbit. She was an ally to the community, believing that love was love and that she'd find her person one day, but she never had anyone in her life like that, so it didn't matter anyway.

Jo Hemsworth never fit in. When Jo's single mother decided to move to a small town toward the end of Jo's junior year, Jo planned not to talk to anyone and just hoped to go to college one day. Never feeling like fitting in, and only in part because of being gay, Jo had no idea Chance was helping to plan a festival and would change Jo's life.

Jaden Hugo had been the girl with two gay dads ever since they adopted her, and she'd been questioning things about herself for a while. When her dads volunteer themselves and her to work at a Pride festival in another town, Jaden is completely taken aback because there was Ruby Simon, the girl who had made it all happen.

On the cusp of their high school graduation, Ruby and Chance were about to leave this place they'd called home and wanted to leave it better than they found it. In planning this first Pride event for their community, their lives also end up changing for the better.

To contact the author or for any additional information, visit: **https://nicolepyland.com**

Cover design: Victoria Cooper Art

BY THE AUTHOR

Stand-alone books:

- The Fire

- The Moments

- The Disappeared

- Reality Check

- Love Forged

- The Show Must Go On

- The Meet Cute Café

- Pride Festival

Chicago Series:

- Introduction – Fresh Start

- Book #1 – The Best Lines

- Book #2 – Just Tell Her

- Book #3 – Love Walked into The Lantern

- Series Finale – What Happened After

San Francisco Series:

- Book #1 – Checking the Right Box

- Book #2 – Macon's Heart

- Book #3 – This Above All

- Series Finale – What Happened After

Tahoe Series:

- Book #1 – Keep Tahoe Blue

- Book #2 – Time of Day

- Book #3 – The Perfect View

- Book #4 – Begin Again

- Series Finale – What Happened After

Sports Series:

- Book #1 – Always More

- Book #2 – A Shot at Gold

- Book #3 – The Unexpected Dream

- Book #4 – Finding a Keeper

Celebrities Series:

- Book #1 – No After You

- Book #2 – All the Love Songs

- Book #3 – Midnight Tradition

- Book #4 – Path Forward

- Series Finale – What Happened After

Boston Series:

- Book #1 – Let Go

- Book #2 – The Right Fit

- Book #3 – All Good Plans

- Book #4 – Around the World

- Series Finale – What Happened After

CONTENTS

CHAPTER 1

"Miss Simon, we appreciate the dedication here, and your presentation was very thorough and well done, but we simply cannot commit the resources."

"What if I can get them myself?" Ruby asked.

"Your budget doesn't account for–"

"I get it. I'm a kid, right?" Ruby interjected. "You can't see me actually having everything I put in that presentation worked out. But it is; you can ask my mom and my dad. They worked it out with me. The budget is spot on. I know we could go over – most people go over budget – but I'm prepared to put in the work, and we can make up any overages with the volunteers and fundraisers."

"You'd have to get the police force to–"

"Volunteer their time," Ruby interrupted again. "I know. I can do that."

"It's April, Miss Simon," a man next to the woman sitting in the middle said.

"I know."

"And you're a high school senior – you have a couple months of school, and then you graduate. Shouldn't you be focused on school and your summer plans?"

"These *are* my summer plans. I don't leave for college until the end of August. I'm already in. All I have left to do there is pick out my classes. And I'm getting As in my high school ones – I have the time for this."

"Miss Simon, you want to plan a major event for the city that would take place in June. Why did you only bring this to the town council in April?"

"I tried to get on the agenda for January, February, and March, but I kept getting denied. The only reason I got on the agenda tonight is that my dad put the request in his name. That's right, isn't it? You thought *he'd* be bringing something up tonight."

"Yes, Miss Simon," the woman in the middle replied. "And we love that you have a passion for your city, but we won't be able to accommodate this request."

"We've never had anything like this here," Ruby said, feeling defeated now. Then, she sighed and added, "I came out to my family when I was fourteen years old, and I was terrified. This town is small, and I didn't think I'd be welcome here anymore because of something I couldn't even change. My parents have supported me, though, and they never once made me feel like they wished I were different than who I am." She paused and turned to her mother and father, who were sitting in the front row, smiling at her. "I know I'm not alone here – I know people like me exist in this town. And some of them might be scared, like I was. They might think they can't be who they are or that they won't be loved anymore, but for the past four years, I've felt loved by this community. No one here has made me feel like I'm no longer welcome or less than someone else. I know this isn't San Francisco, LA, or New York. I know it's a tiny community on the edge of a lake with a bunch of farms, and some people are barely making ends meet, but there aren't any resources here for people like me. If we have a Pride event, I can get people here from other towns. I can bring them here, and they can – I don't know – show others that there's a world out there with people in it like them. They could talk to people who have gone through what they might be too afraid to go through. They could have fun, too. And I think you can see in the budget and profit analysis I did there that if we go with my plan, we would actually bring in revenue to the town. So, if you can't see why we could use something like this for people like me and for the people who support people like me, maybe you can see it from that perspective."

No one said anything for a moment. Then, the woman in the middle covered her microphone and leaned over to the man at her right. They talked quietly for a minute before she turned to the woman at her left, and they did the same. Then, she uncovered the microphone, cleared her throat, and looked toward Ruby's father.

"Mr. Simon, would you please stand with your daughter?"

Her father stood, buttoned his tailored suit jacket, and walked over to Ruby. He winked at her and placed his hand on the small of her back, giving it a little pat.

"Mr. Simon, while Ruby is technically an adult, she *is* eighteen and your dependent."

"Yes, ma'am," he said in his deep baritone.

"If we allow this, would you be supervising the effort?"

"Her mother and I both will, yes. We are both very proud of Ruby. She works incredibly hard in school, earns straight As, participates in academic clubs, and has already gotten into a great university. While she could be coasting for the rest of the school year and for her summer, she's decided she wants to contribute to the town she loves, and we want to support her however we can," he said.

"And the overages?" the woman asked.

"If there are any, Ruby has a plan to host several fundraisers, and her mother and I are prepared to donate as well if more funds are required," he replied, smiling down at Ruby.

"It's a short turnaround," the man on the town council said, coughing immediately after. "You're talking about the middle of June. It's April."

"We're aware, and we've done a lot of the prep work already. We just need the go-ahead and the permits, and we can continue from here," Ruby said, wanting to speak for herself.

"We?"

"My best friend, Chance, and I," she replied, pointing to Chance, who was sitting next to Ruby's mother. "She's been helping, too. We've made calls, asked for people to help, and she's willing to help herself."

They turned to Chance, who waved a little shyly up at them.

"You'll need a lot more than just the two of you," the woman at the left said.

"I know. I've got other kids from school, too. The list of people who have signed up is in the back of the presentation, and I can get more. Once we have approval, I'll get people from neighboring towns. And there's that private school in Monroe, too – I bet I can get some of those kids to help."

They turned to each other again, and Ruby swallowed. Her dad placed his hand on her shoulder, squeezed it, and gave her a reassuring smile.

"We'll consider the plan and have an answer for you by the end of the week, since you'd need to get started soon," the woman in the middle announced.

"Really?" Ruby said, sounding way too excited.

"Yes, Miss Simon." The woman chuckled a little. "Friday end of business, Mr. Simon?"

"Sounds good," Ruby's father said, nodding.

"Very well. We're adjourned."

Ruby and her father backed away from the microphone.

"What does that mean?" Ruby asked him.

"Well, I don't want you to get your hopes up, but I think it's good news."

"Yeah?" Ruby asked as her mother approached them.

"I'm proud of you, honey," her mom said, pulling her in for a hug.

"Mom, we're at the town council," Ruby argued softly, begrudgingly hugging her back.

"You kind of kicked ass just now," Chance said, holding up her hand for a high-five.

"Did I? I hope so. I interrupted her, like, four times," Ruby replied, giving her a high-five and running her hand through her short brown hair.

"I think she liked it. It shows you really care about this thing."

"I *do* care about it," Ruby told her.

"I know that. I've been with you since the beginning, Si-mon," Chance replied, smiling at her. "Come on. Your parents are taking us out for pizza to celebrate, and *I'm* getting extra pepperoni."

Ruby knew this was a long shot, but she had to try. When she was twelve years old, she'd figured out that she liked girls in the way she was supposed to like boys, and she spent the next two years hiding that part of herself from the world. She'd been so worried then that she'd lose her parents, who had been God-fearing churchgoers their entire lives, or that her brother, who was two years older, wouldn't talk to her anymore, and that her best friend wouldn't want to be friends anymore, either. On top of that, Ruby worried that her town would disown her, and she'd spent her entire life in this place.

She'd told her parents on her fourteenth birthday that she was a lesbian. They'd had a bunch of questions for her, but they'd never told her that it was a phase, that she was wrong, a sinner, would not have the life they wanted for her, or anything like that. Instead, they told her they loved her and that they'd always be there for her. She'd cried that night, but they had been happy tears, and then her sixteen-year-old brother had told her that if anyone gave her a hard time about it, he'd kick their ass.

Chance had been next on her list and had basically said the same thing. She'd hugged Ruby and told her she loved her and that they'd be friends no matter what. Now, they were about to graduate and move into an off-campus apartment together at the same college. The one thing Ruby wanted to do before she left, though, was host the very first Pride event in her small community. And she only needed two of those three people to agree to let her.

CHAPTER 2

"So, I know it's not a big parade with feather boas and half-naked people running around," Ruby began in front of the gathered crowd. "But it's a big start, and people love festivals. We'll have rides, games, raffles, tons of food, and most importantly, booths sponsored by several LGBTQ+ charities and organizations. We'll even have a helpline set up and people manning it for anyone who might just need someone to talk to. That will be inside the community center and is obviously confidential. Anyone who wants to volunteer their time would have to go through training beginning right away. I have a sign-up sheet for that, and the center that's running it has representatives here to talk to you in a bit. It's going to be fun, and that's important, but it *is* a Pride event, so we want to keep that as our focus."

"You mean, a bunch of rainbows all over the place?" her brother asked, and he appeared to be serious.

"No," Ruby replied. "It means that the booths where people can get information are more important than the game where you can win a big stuffed animal."

Chance laughed, as did several of the others. Ruby had heard back from the town council that they'd approved her carnival event idea and that they would issue the permits for her to use the open field next to the old community center that had seen better days. It was great news, but it also meant that now, the real work got started. Ruby went on to explain that they'd already contracted a carnival company to provide the rides and games, but that left the food, raffles, music, other events, and the booths to the group of about fifty people currently sitting in brown metal folding chairs in the community center's multi-purpose room.

Chance looked around the space and saw several kids from school that she knew. Their class was only about two hundred people, and the school itself was a junior-senior school, which meant it held seventh grade through twelfth and only had about fifteen hundred students in all. It was the only public school in the town, and the nearest private school was in Monroe, which was about an hour away.

Chance wasn't surprised to see a few kids that looked to be about her age that she didn't recognize there. They'd likely come from one of the schools in other cities, which meant that Ruby had already reached out and asked for volunteers. Her best friend had always been a joiner and had been on a mission to make things easier for anyone who comes after her at just about anything. Hell, Ruby had had a locker door that squeaked sophomore year, and on their last day of class, she'd fixed the damn thing for the kid that got it the following year.

Chance probably would have left it alone. She also wasn't a big natural joiner. She was much better at home, with a good book, or just scrolling on her phone, watching everyone else live their lives, but being best friends with an extravert who loved to be in the world every way she could, meant that Chance often tagged along, and she'd been made better for it. Had she and Ruby not met in kindergarten and became friends, Chance probably wouldn't have more than a couple of friends and would have watched these years pass her by.

"Can I sit here?"

Chance looked up and noticed a girl about her age, with short blonde hair that was mussed on top of her head as if she'd just woken up like that, left the house, and it was okay with her that it was curled and sticking a little all over the place.

"Oh, sure," Chance replied, moving her purse from the empty chair next to her and putting it in her lap instead.

"Thanks," she replied, sitting down. "Sorry, I'm late. I had to walk when my car didn't start."

Chance turned back to her and noticed that the girl *did* look a little sweaty.

"No problem," Chance replied.

"Okay. Any questions?" Ruby asked, forcing Chance's attention away from the girl who was wiping her brow with her probably equally sweaty forearm.

"Shit. I missed all of it," the girl said, probably more to herself than Chance.

"Thank you, everyone. I can't wait to see this whole vision come to life," Ruby added.

Everyone applauded, including Chance, who then turned to the girl again, more fully this time.

"I can fill you in if you want," she offered.

"Yeah?" the girl said back, looking hopeful, running a hand through that hair.

"Sure. I'm Chance." Chance held out her hand for the girl to shake.

"Oh. I'm Jo," she replied. "And I don't know if you want me to shake your hand... Sweat, remember? It's like a hundred degrees, and it's April. How do you guys deal with this?"

Chance lowered her hand and smiled at Jo instead.

"Are you from Monroe?"

"No. I just moved *here*, actually," Jo said. "My mom got a new job. We got in last weekend."

"Oh, do you go to *Roosevelt*?"

"Not yet. I start on Monday," Jo replied. "We took the week to get moved in. It's just the two of us, and we didn't have movers."

"Senior?"

"Junior," Jo said.

"You had to move in the middle of the school year?"

"Yeah, it sucks," Jo replied. "But my mom needed the work, and I'm along for the ride. You?"

"My mom?"

"No," Jo said, laughing a little, and Chance didn't understand why, but that laugh sounded sweet to her. "Junior? Senior?"

"Senior, thankfully. I am about to graduate," Chance shared. "And finally go to college. I can't wait. I have this summer program that starts in July – it's an internship, really, and it's unpaid, but I can't wait. I'm kind of already packing, and I think I might be offending my parents."

Jo laughed again and said, "I'm sure they get it."

"So… You want to volunteer for this?" Chance asked, motioning around the room.

"Yeah. I heard about it yesterday when I was at the grocery store with my mom and saw the flyer. I swear, I planned to leave with plenty of time, but my car is from the last century, and no matter what I tried, it wouldn't start. I would have borrowed my mom's, but she's working, so I had to walk. I tried to run part of the way, but the heat got to me."

"Do you need some water?" Chance asked, chuckling at her.

"Probably."

"Come on. My dad and I brought a bunch of bottled water for everyone. There are some snacks, too," Chance added.

"Your dad is cool with you being here?" Jo asked, standing up.

Chance stood as well and said, "Yeah, of course. He adores Ruby. Sometimes, I think he would've preferred her as his daughter, but yeah, he's cool with whatever: gay, straight, bi, anything in between. My mom is, too."

"Ruby?" Jo asked.

"Ruby." Chance pointed at Ruby, who was talking to two men. "My best friend. She's the one organizing this whole thing."

"Ah," Jo said, looking at Ruby now. "She's our age, right?"

"Yeah. Well, she's a senior."

Chance walked them over to the table they'd set up earlier where they'd placed the waters and a few bags of chips, granola bars, and a couple of other items they'd found at the store yesterday. Jo grabbed a bottle immediately and took a long drink.

"How far *did* you walk?" Chance asked, smiling at her.

"It felt like ten miles," Jo stated. "But it's really only three, I think. I ran for about a mile of that, though."

"You *really* wanted to be here," Chance replied.

"Yeah, it's something I wanted to do. Where we just moved from, there weren't any Pride events. And I doubt anyone in that town has even heard of Pride," she said.

"Small town?"

"Yeah, smaller than this one. As far as I know, I was the only gay kid. I'm sure I wasn't, obviously, but I was the only one that was out, and it wasn't exactly a warm welcome when I was outed."

"Outed?" Chance asked. "You didn't get to–"

"Come out on my own? No," Jo replied, finishing the water and tossing it into the recycling bin in the corner. "It's a long story, and probably one for another time."

"Sure," Chance said softly, remembering how Ruby had come out to her.

It was such a personal thing for someone, and Chance hated that Jo hadn't had the chance to tell people when and how she wanted. Chance also wanted to know more, but she didn't press any further. It was up to Jo to tell her the story if she ever wanted to.

"Well, if you need someone to sit next to at lunch on Monday, Ruby and I are always at the table in the corner. You can sit with us if you want," she offered, changing the subject.

Jo smiled and said, "Yeah, that would be cool. Thanks."

"I'll fill you in on what you missed and introduce you to Ruby. She'll have at least ten assignments for you."

Jo laughed again.

CHAPTER 3

Jo wasn't sure she would like the new school, but it had to be better than her old one. That one had been smaller, and she'd felt so alone there. Never really knowing where she fit was only partly because she liked girls the way boys did – Jo never felt like one of the rest of the girls. She'd hated having long hair and had begged her mother to let her cut it short for years before her mom had finally given in and let her essentially lop it off and leave it in the mess it currently resembled. Jo's breasts had also come in early but had stopped at barely a B-cup while the other girls were continuing to develop. Her hips were still pretty straight, and she was on the thin side.

On top of all that, Jo didn't really fit in with the boys, either. She wasn't a big fan of athletics, cars, and building muscles in the weight room like the guys in her school were. She also didn't like how some of them talked about the girls they liked, wanted to have sex with, or *had* had sex with already. Their hormones had gotten the best of them, and Jo found all of that annoying and, sometimes, disgusting.

Not fitting in with the girls *or* the boys had left her feeling even more alone than being the only lesbian she knew at school. When she looked at herself in the mirror, she wasn't sure what it all meant. To Jo, it made more sense that she was neither, but trying to explain to her mother that she liked girls, after being outed at school, had been hard enough. Explaining that she might also not identify as a girl or a boy would be something different altogether, and since Jo was still trying to figure it out herself, she didn't think she needed to put it on her mom just yet.

Jo was grateful she'd made that long walk to the community center on Saturday because she'd met Chance and Ruby there. Chance had been kind to her, had walked her through the plan for the Pride event, and had even laughed at some of Jo's

11

lame jokes. Ruby had been pretty busy, so Jo hadn't spent much time with her that day, but when she'd spied them laughing together as the two girls walked to their table in the school cafeteria, Jo had taken the opportunity to join them. She'd sat with them every day for the week and found that she really liked them.

One reason she liked Ruby was that she'd never talked to another out lesbian before, and while they hadn't exactly talked about anything related to their coming-out journeys, it was nice just knowing that someone else understood, someone else would support her and be there to talk to if Jo needed. Jo liked talking to Chance, too, though, and not just at lunch. They didn't have any classes together, but they did have classes next to each other two times during the day, which meant that Jo could wait outside her class door and see Chance when she came out of hers.

They'd walked to their lockers together Tuesday, Wednesday, Thursday, and Friday of the previous week. Now, they were lugging food donations for the festival into the old barn they were using for storage until the event.

"These are just the first two trucks. We have a bunch more coming in the next few weeks," Chance told her. "I didn't realize how much physical labor would be involved in this. I think Ruby thinks I need to work out or something. My muscles don't exist, I guess." She dropped the twenty-four pack of bottled water onto the stack of the others and flexed her left arm. "See? Nothing."

Jo cleared her throat rather loudly and said, "I think it's fine... You're fine." Then, she dropped her own bottled water on top of Chance's, and they turned to go back outside to get another. "Shouldn't there be a cart or something we can use?"

"There are a few of them, but they've got them already," Chance replied, pointing to people loading in what looked like heavy boxes. "I think that's funnel cake stuff, and there's canned fruit filling – that stuff is heavier than what we're lifting."

"Yeah, I guess we can carry a few more waters," Jo replied, wiping her brow. "Still, it's so damn hot here."

Chance laughed, and it brightened her entire face. Her long brown hair had been pulled back into a ponytail and looked a little frazzled with the humidity in the air, and her light-blue eyes were directed at the semi-truck, which had brought the first deliveries of non-perishables for the festival. Chance also had a few freckles on her cheeks and a smattering on her nose that had Jo going weak in the knees. For freckles; Jo was going weak in the knees for Chance's freaking freckles. What in the hell was wrong with her?

"So, how was your first week?" Chance asked as they both picked up another case.

"Fine, I guess. Thank you for letting me sit with you guys."

"Of course. You don't have to thank us."

"It's harder than I thought, being the new girl."

"Yeah?" Chance asked.

"I hated my old school, so I thought I'd be good wherever. And this place is fine; it's just hard showing up at basically the end of the year. You guys are a little ahead of where I was there, and there wasn't any room in *Algebra II*, so they stuck me in *Pre-Calculus* – I don't know anything about pre-calculus."

"They won't move you to algebra?" Chance asked.

"I asked my mom to talk to them, and she said she would, but I don't know if they'll let me move yet."

"That sucks. I'm taking calc, and I'm getting a B in it, so if you need help, I can maybe tutor you or something."

"I'd have to learn about seven months of pre-calc in, like, a week in order to pass an upcoming quiz – I'm a lost cause." Jo sighed. "On the upside, though, I'm in *Advanced English* here, which is great. We didn't have it at my old school, and I love reading and writing, so I think I'll be good there."

"You like to write?" Chance asked as she dropped the water down.

"Sometimes, yeah."

"What do you write?"

"Just in my journal and maybe a few poems and stuff. I've tried a couple of short stories; nothing too serious."

"That's cool. I love to read. And I'm not much of a writer,

but I read just about anything," Chance said. "Maybe I can read something of yours one day."

"Oh, it's not good. I just like to do it." Jo dropped her water. "I think it helps when you feel like you're... the only one."

Chance turned to her and asked, "The only gay one?"

"That too," Jo replied softly. "Being a teenager just kind of sucks. You're in between, you know? We're not kids anymore, but we're not adults yet, either. We're figuring things out – who we are, who we want to be, what we want to do – and it's just a lot."

"I hear that," Chance said, sighing.

"Hey," Ruby said, walking over to them, holding on to the clipboard.

"Oh, no... She has a pen in her hand and the clipboard – we're about to get more work," Chance joked.

"Yes, you are," Ruby replied, smiling at her. "Can you do me a favor, and supervise the art?"

"Art?" Jo asked even though Ruby had been talking to Chance.

"We're doing this little film festival, too. Well, basically, we're using a room in the community center to show some queer movies, and the hallway will display some queer art," Ruby explained. "I thought Chance could head over there and work with the vendor who's putting it all on for us. They just want to look at the space today. They're donating their services and have lined up artists and movies for us already."

"Oh, sure," Chance replied. "Happy to get out of the heat and be done with physical labor."

"Can *I* go?" Jo asked, hopeful.

"Actually, I was hoping you'd come work with me. Can you help get the phone lines set up? It's basically plugging things in and making sure it all works."

"I guess, yeah."

"It's inside," Ruby said, trying to sell it to Sher.

Jo laughed and said, "Then, definitely."

In Ruby's car, they made their way to the community center, which was really just on the other side of the parking lot.

Chance was in the passenger seat, and Jo sat behind Ruby in the back. Watching these two friends who had known each other forever interact was fascinating – Jo hadn't ever had a best friend. They seemed to complete each other's sentences nearly all of the time and laughed a lot. She'd noticed that at school, too, but it seemed like these two were always laughing. When they got to the center, Chance went one way to work with the art vendor, and Ruby and Jo went the other way to work with the helpline people.

"Why are we getting this done now?" Jo asked when they entered the room. "It's only April."

"They have to train people, and they actually call in to do that, so we want this all working as soon as possible."

"Oh," Jo uttered, realizing she hadn't thought of that.

About thirty minutes later, she and Ruby had gotten tables in position, along with the phones that now needed to be tested. She'd caught Chance in the hall a few times, too. Once, she'd smiled and waved at Jo, causing Jo to smile and wave awkwardly back.

"How are you liking it here so far?" Ruby asked.

"Oh, it's fine," she replied. "It's only been a couple of weeks."

"Making friends yet?"

"You and Chance."

"No one else?" Ruby asked, lifting an eyebrow.

"Not yet, no. I'm still trying to get caught up with my classes and stuff."

"Can I help at all? I'm good in school."

"Oh, thank you. I'm sure I'll be okay. Chance offered to help me with pre-calc, and I think I'm fine with the other stuff."

"Chance is getting a B in calc," Ruby stated.

"Yeah, that's what she said," Jo confirmed.

"I'm getting an A," Ruby added.

"Maybe both of you can help me at lunch or something."

"Yeah, sure," Ruby said.

"I'm trying to get into *Algebra II* anyway, so I might not need it," Jo told her.

"Hey, can I ask you something?" Ruby asked her, standing still for the first time all day from what Jo had noticed.

"Sure."

"Are you into Chance?"

Jo tried not to look surprised at the question, but she was no actor, so she was certain Ruby could tell. When she added that to the blush that was creeping up her neck, Ruby didn't even need her to confirm; she just nodded at Jo.

"She's straight, you know?"

"Oh, I…" Jo began without knowing where she'd end.

"I don't mean to, like, put you off or something. I could just tell you were crushing pretty hard."

"So, you two are really just friends?" Jo asked. "I wasn't sure."

"Yeah. I love Chance, but not into her or anything."

"Plus, she's straight?"

"Well, yeah," Ruby replied. "It's not really just straight, though – Chance hasn't identified as anything, technically. When I came out, she was awesome about it, and she told me she doesn't believe that anyone is one hundred percent purely *anything* in life, including sexual orientation. So, take that for what you want, but she's never told me she was interested in any girls or anything."

"Okay," Jo replied, embarrassed now.

"If you want to ask her something or whatever, you can," Ruby added. "I just wanted you to know."

"No, I'm good with… friends. I kind of need them right now, so I don't want to cause any problems." Jo paused before asking, "You won't say anything to Chance, will you?"

"That you like her?" Ruby asked, shaking her head. "No."

"Thanks." Jo looked out the open door again just as Chance walked past with an older woman.

Chance turned again, offering Jo another smile. Jo smiled back and gave her another wave. Chance laughed silently and walked on.

CHAPTER 4

Ruby watched the two men approach. She'd talked to them a couple of weeks ago about helping out with the event and getting their daughter involved. They'd been together for over twenty years, and something about that gave Ruby hope for her own future. Married for the past six, they'd been able to adopt before then and had gotten their daughter, Jaden, when she was five, if Ruby remembered their conversation correctly. She expected to see maybe a twelve-year-old or something and had planned a few tasks for someone that age to do this weekend, but when the two men parted while still on their way to Ruby, she didn't see a twelve-year-old – she saw a beautiful young woman.

"Hi, Ruby," Neil greeted.

"Hi," she replied, unable to take her eyes off of the girl standing at his right.

"Ruby, this is our daughter, Jaden," Sergio added, placing an arm over Jaden's shoulders. "We thought you'd be able to put her to work today."

"Yeah, sure," Ruby said, swallowing and staring down at her clipboard at the list of menial tasks she'd made for Jaden. "Um... you can just help me today."

"Okay," Jaden said softly. "With what, though?"

"I have your dads volunteering to get trained for the help-line. Do you maybe want to go to the field and help me measure things?"

"Measure?"

"Yeah, I have to measure where everything will go. The food tents and the booths; that kind of stuff. We want to rent all the right sizes the first time, obviously."

"Okay. Yeah, that sounds easy enough," Jaden replied.

"We'll see you later, honey," Neil said to his daughter.

"Bye," Jaden replied as the men walked off. "Sorry about this," she said to Ruby.

"About what?"

"My dads, sticking you with me," Jaden replied.

She had blonde hair that was about shoulder-length and slightly wavy and these blue eyes that were slightly darker than Chance's really light ones. Jaden's skin was also near caramel and smooth. How she didn't have a single pimple on her face was beyond Ruby because Ruby still dealt with regular, annoying flare-ups.

"Oh. No, it's cool. I need all the help I can get," she replied, finally gathering her thoughts. "Do you not want to be here, though? They told me the day of the meeting that you were in-terested in–"

"Yeah, I am," Jaden interrupted. "I want to help. I just don't want you to think that you have to keep an eye on me or something. I don't want to get in your way. This is cool; what you're doing."

"It is?" Ruby asked.

Jaden chuckled and said, "Yeah, it is. I've got two dads, so I think Pride is pretty important. And, well, I don't exactly know... you know... where I... fit in."

Ruby didn't want to assume she knew what Jaden meant by that, so she just nodded.

"You're in charge, so does that mean..."

"Oh, yeah – I'm gay," Ruby replied. "Girls only for me." She internally chastised herself for that stupid remark.

Jaden laughed again and said, "Cool. Girls are cool."

"Yeah," Ruby added, wondering what that statement meant.

"Anyway... Measuring things?"

"Sure. Let's go," Ruby said. "I'll drive."

They climbed into Ruby's car, which had been a gift from her parents on her sixteenth birthday, and drove the short dis-tance to the other side of the field where she needed to measure first. Ordering tents was first on her list now that other things had already started moving forward. Her dad had three tent companies offering steep discounts to be a sponsor, but their inventories for the weekend of the festival were all different, so she wanted to use her math skills to see if she could figure out what they needed before they placed their order.

"So, your dad said you go to that school in Monroe," Ruby spoke when she popped her trunk, looking for her supplies.

"Yeah, *Monroe Prep*," Jaden said. "You go here, I take it?"

"Yeah, *Roosevelt Junior-Senior*," she replied, pulling out the measuring tape and chalk line her dad had lent her for the day.

"What year?" Jaden asked.

"Senior. You?"

"Senior," Jaden said.

"College?"

"Yeah. State for me." She shrugged. "I didn't really care much where I went. I don't know what I want to do yet, so I thought I'd go somewhere cheap until I do and not waste a bunch of money. What about you?"

"Dexter University," Ruby replied, closing the trunk.

"That's a good school."

"Yeah, it is. My best friend and I both got in, so we're going to share an apartment off-campus. We could do the dorms, but our parents said they want us to be totally focused on school and not work, at least for our freshman year, so they're footing the bill."

"That's nice. I'll be dorming it," Jaden said.

"That's cool, too, though. You'll get a roomie and have events there and stuff, so you'll meet new people easily," Ruby said.

"I guess, yeah," Jaden replied as they walked onto the field. "So, what gave you the idea for this thing?"

"Oh, I don't know. I guess I was scrolling social and saw a bunch of ads for Pride events around the world last year. I started talking to my parents about how we'd never do anything like that here, and my dad dared me to try." She laughed. "So, I did."

"And here we are," Jaden said as they stopped walking. "That's pretty cool, Ruby."

Ruby stared at her and replied, "It's not cool until it's happening. Right now, it's a lot of work."

"Well, I'm here. How can I help?"

"Just hold one end of this thing," Ruby told her. "I've got table and equipment measurements and stuff, and I just want to be really thorough. If anything is wrong, it's on me, you know? This is too important to me to mess up." She handed Jaden the measuring tape.

"Can I ask you something?"

"Yeah."

"That best friend you mentioned..."

"Yeah?" Ruby asked, walking backward with the end of the tape.

"Just a best friend?"

"Oh. Chance? Yeah. We get that a lot, but just friends. Have you met her?"

"No, I've only met *you* so far."

"She's cool. I'll introduce you to her later," Ruby said, tripping on a rock but catching herself before she fell.

"You okay over there?" Jaden asked, laughing.

"You try walking backward," she replied, laughing back.

"How long have you known?"

"Known what?"

"The gay thing," Jaden said.

"Since I was about twelve. Came out at fourteen."

"That's cool," Jaden replied.

Then, Ruby stopped walking and asked, "What's the measurement?"

"Oh," Jaden said, looking down before she read it off to her. "Is that good?"

"Yeah, that's what I thought it would be. Let's get the other side now," she suggested. "You said earlier that you weren't sure where you... fit in."

"Yeah, I like guys," Jaden replied. "I've only dated guys."

"Oh," Ruby uttered, a bit surprised and very disappointed.

"But I…" Jaden paused before saying, "Recently, I've been thinking I might like girls, too."

Ruby let go of the measuring tape and watched as it snapped all the way back to Jaden, who looked up at her and laughed.

"*That's* a reaction," she said.

"Sorry," Ruby replied.

"No, it's okay."

"Do your dads know?"

"Why do you think they asked me to come here and help?" She walked over to Ruby and handed her the measuring tape. "I've never been on a date with a girl or anything, though."

"I don't think you need to go on a date to know if you're into girls. I'd never been on a date when *I* knew, at least," Ruby replied.

"And what about now?"

"Now?" Ruby asked.

"Do you date now? It's just a small town… Monroe is a little bigger, so I know there's one girl out at my school, but I'm not into *her* at all."

Ruby laughed and asked, "Not your type?"

"Emo. Cool, I guess, but not my thing."

"What *is* your thing?" Ruby asked, wanting to know more than if her measurements for this field would work out.

"I don't know yet," Jaden replied, smiling softly at her.

"Will you let me know when you do?" Ruby asked.

"You're really interested in knowing that?"

"Yes," Ruby said.

"Even though I've never…" Jaden said. "You know."

"We could…"

Jaden's eyes widened.

"No, not that," Ruby said. "I mean, I don't even know that I know what you meant just now. Did you mean, like, that you've never dated a girl or that you've never…" She leaned in and whispered, "Had sex with one?"

Jaden laughed softly and said, "Well, technically, I've never done either, but I meant the date thing."

21

"Oh, cool," Ruby said. "We could do that."

"We could?" Jaden looked a little surprised.

"Or not. We could hang out. Like, there's a movie, and we could… be there."

"At the movie?" Jaden asked.

"Yeah, we could watch it together."

"That *is* what people usually do there, yes," Jaden teased.

"Do you want to?"

"My dads were right."

"Huh?" Ruby asked.

"They said I'd like you," Jaden replied, shaking her head. "I can't believe they were right."

"They told you that you'd–"

"They also said that you were cute," Jaden interrupted.

"Cute?"

"They were right about that, too," Jaden told her.

Ruby could only smile.

CHAPTER 5

Chance had taken two advanced placement classes this year. One of them was AP English, and the other was AP European History. Both of them had tests this week. She needed to score a four or a five to then test out of the general education requirements next year. The entire school year had been spent prepping for this week, and now, she just needed to buckle down and score well.

Chance had finished the history test the previous day and felt pretty good about it. She figured she at least had a three, but likely, a four. The English test was the one she really cared about. She couldn't imagine having to sit through a full year of freshman composition and was hoping she could at least get a four or a five to get her moved into a sophomore-level course instead.

The exam itself wasn't all that challenging, but it involved four essay questions about books, and there were over a hundred books that the exam could reference. She hadn't read every single one of them, but she'd at least studied the SparkNotes for all of them. The fourth essay was an open question, and she could use any book or books to answer it. That one, Chance felt a little better about, and hours later, when she left the library where the students had taken the test, she could finally breathe a sigh of relief.

"Hey," Jo said.

"Oh, hey. What are you still doing here?" Chance asked.

It was after four, and school had let out over an hour ago.

"Oh, Ruby said you were taking your test today, so I thought I'd wait and see how you did."

Chance smiled and said, "You waited for me?"

"Well, I was doing some homework, too, but yeah," she replied.

"You didn't have to do that. Is Ruby still here, too?"

"No, she went over to the community center. She was on the phone with Jaden, so I couldn't get much info out of her."

"Jaden, huh?" Chance said, lifting an eyebrow as they walked down the hall.

"Yeah. She seems cool," Jo replied, kind of tossing her hair around on her head.

"She does, yeah. They have a date this weekend." Chance stopped at her locker and twisted the lock around a few times until it opened. "Jaden's never been out with another girl before, so Ruby's super nervous."

"Oh, me too," Jo said.

"*You're* nervous about *their* date?" Chance shoved her books inside the locker.

"No, I meant that I've never been on a date with a girl," Jo replied, biting her lower lip.

"Really?"

"I told you it wasn't easy back home and that I was the only one I knew who was out," Jo reminded.

"I know. I guess I just hadn't thought about the whole dating thing."

Jo shrugged.

"So, did you like any of the girls at your old school?" Chance asked, closing her locker after packing her backpack and slinging it over her shoulder.

"One last year, but I wasn't in love with her or anything. She was nice and pretty."

"What was her name?" Chance asked, nodding for Jo to start walking.

"Tiff."

"Tiff?" Chance laughed.

"Yeah. Why? Tiffany, but she went by Tiff."

"Just the way you said that sounded like you were sneezing."

"Oh," Jo said, laughing now. "No sneezing. That's just her name."

"Is your name short for Josephine?"

"Yeah," Jo replied. "My mom was a big *Little Women* fan. Where does Chance come from?"

They turned the corner and headed to the front glass doors of the school.

"I'm a rainbow baby," Chance replied. "My parents had a miscarriage before I was born. They thought of me as their second *chance* to have a baby, so they named me Chance."

"Sorry, I didn't know," Jo said, opening the door for her to walk through first.

"Thank you," Chance said. "Where's your car?"

"I walked today. It was acting up again this morning. My mom and I are going to jump it when she gets off from work."

"Do you need a ride home?" Chance asked.

"No, it's okay; I can walk. It's only ninety-five degrees today."

Chance laughed and said, "Come on. I can take you home. Or, if you want, you can come to the festival grounds with me. I'm supposed to drop off some stuff for Ruby that she's got in my trunk."

"Can I help?"

"I'm sure you could, but we could also just drop and run."

"We can?" Jo asked, laughing.

"We can go to *Carver's* and have ice cream after. Then, I can drop you off if you want."

"I haven't been there yet," Jo said.

"Oh, you have to go, then. It's amazing. The Carvers are both, like, eighty years old, and they've owned this place forever. It's so good."

"Okay. I'm in," Jo told her, smiling as they arrived at Chance's car.

Ruby was busy at the community center, so Chance left the boxes from her trunk with Mrs. Simon, who had walked outside just as Chance and Jo had arrived. She waved them off quickly, too.

"She's on the warpath," Mrs. Simon said of her daughter. "Save yourselves," she teased.

"What happened?"

"Three volunteers dropped out because their families decided to go on vacation during the festival, so Ruby's just disappointed, but it'll be fine. Seriously, you two should go have some fun, though; while you still can." She winked at them.

Chance and Jo climbed back into the car and blasted the AC.

"Ice cream?" Jo asked her. "I'm buying."

"Then, I'm having two scoops and extra toppings," Chance joked.

"You can have whatever you want," Jo told her.

Chance turned to her, wondering where that had come from, but was only met with Jo's warm eyes and soft smile. Chance smiled back and drove them toward *Carver's*. After the short drive and ordering, they took their ice cream to one of the red metal round tables with a blue umbrella over it and sat down next to each other to eat before everything melted in the heat.

"So, how are you feeling about school almost being over?" Jo asked after a minute.

"Good. I think I got a four on the test today, at least."

"Why didn't Ruby take it with you?" Jo asked, taking a bite of her chocolate ice cream.

"She took this one last year. I couldn't because I had another class that was offered at the same time that I needed." Chance took a bite of her two scoops of vanilla with chocolate syrup and sprinkles. "Ruby is really smart. She took three AP classes last year, and three this year, too. She'll be able to skip at least five classes. She could even graduate college a semester early if all goes according to her plan."

"What's *your* plan?"

"I have no idea." Chance laughed a little. "I guess, go to college, find my major and career out of it, maybe have a little fun while I'm there, and then get a job doing... something."

"I guess that's mine, too," Jo said.

"Yeah?"

"I have no idea what I want to do yet." Jo took another bite of her ice cream. "I'm seventeen... How am I supposed to know what I'll want in, like, ten years?"

"No clue," Chance replied. "I'm eighteen, and I have no idea, either. I think I want to do something with English. I just don't know that I want to teach, and I don't want to write, really, so I guess I'll take a few classes and hope to figure it out."

"I might like to write one day," Jo shared.

"I thought you said you weren't any good," Chance teased, knocking their shoulders together playfully.

"Not yet, but if I go to school for it, I could learn," she said.

Chance nodded and said, "Want to try this?" She pushed her dish of ice cream toward Jo.

"It's vanilla ice cream."

"Says the girl who got plain chocolate," Chance teased, smiling at her.

Jo's expression changed then, and she turned away toward the creek that was next to the small ice cream stand.

"What's wrong?" Chance asked.

"Nothing." Jo turned back, but her face was more serious now.

"Jo, you can tell me."

"I'm okay." She nodded.

"Really? You look like you're about to throw up."

"No," Jo said. "I'm–" She stopped. "This is good ice cream." She pointed her red plastic spoon at her dish.

Chance decided she'd let it go. Jo clearly wasn't ready to talk to her about whatever it was that was bothering her.

"That creek leads to the lake," she said, nodding toward the creek that was really more a light stream when they went without rain for a long time.

"There's a lake here?" Jo asked.

"You didn't know?"

Jo shook her head.

"We can walk there from here if you want. I can just show it to you," Chance offered. "Ruby's family has their house on the water. I'm not so lucky, but I spend the night there a lot, and we go swimming in the lake or in their pool. It's fun. You could come sometime."

"Can we maybe walk there when it's not so hot?" Jo asked, looking as if she was begging Chance with her expression.

Chance laughed and, for whatever reason, ran her hand through Jo's messy hair to push it back a bit from her forehead.

CHAPTER 6

"Hey, honey," her father said.

"Hi," Jaden replied without looking away from the clothes in her closet.

"Going out tonight?"

"Yeah," she said. "Just trying to find something to wear, but my uniforms take over half my closet."

He laughed and said, "How about just a pair of jeans and an old T-shirt? It's going to be a hot night and–"

"Dad, I can't just wear an old t-shirt," she replied.

Then, Jaden flopped her butt on the side of her bed and groaned.

"What's going on, Jade?" he asked, walking more into her room now.

"Nothing. I just wish I liked my clothes."

"You picked out all those clothes." He laughed.

"I know, but nothing I own is right."

"Right for what?" he asked, peering into her closet. "I see a ton of options for a night out with your friends."

"It's–" Jaden stopped herself.

He turned his face to her and gave her a quizzical expression, expecting her to say something else, but Jaden hadn't yet told her dads that she was going on a date with Ruby. They'd been talking every day for a week now. In the morning, one of them would text the other first, and then they'd be off, finding excuses to text throughout the day, sending each other pictures throughout school, messaging updates about classes, and asking each other questions about things like favorite movies, most embarrassing moments, and just about everything else. Jaden had been following Ruby's Instagram posts of the festival progress as well, making sure to like everything to show her support.

Jaden had never been a big fan of talking on the phone. Why talk when she could text? With Ruby, it was different, though. Ruby didn't go to Jaden's school, and she lived about

29

an hour away, so they couldn't easily see each other in person all the time. Besides, Jaden's dads had weeknight rules for her that didn't apply to the non-school nights. They weren't overbearing or anything, but if she was going to spend time with friends, they wanted her home by dinner unless it was school-related. That made it difficult to get to Ruby to help with the festival during the week, which limited their time together.

So, phone calls in the evenings after dinner had become their thing. Ruby would text first to see if dinner was over. Then, Jaden would disappear into her bedroom, and they'd talk for as long as they could, sometimes hanging up to do homework or grab a snack and calling each other right back. Ruby was funny; Jaden found herself laughing constantly. She was smart, too. Ruby had already gotten into a great school and didn't have to focus much on the end of her senior year. According to Ruby, there were three classes that no matter how she scored on her final exams, she'd still get at least a B. Jaden still had to focus on some of her classes, or she risked failing and being held back.

Private school was different. She'd long suspected that her fathers, who weren't rich men, put her in *Monroe Prep* as a way of somehow making up for the mother who'd dropped her off with a note in her tiny hand at a hospital one day when she was four years old, leaving her there. Jaden didn't remember much from the time before her dads adopted her, but she knew she was better off now than she would have been. Her fathers loved her, and when she'd first mentioned to them that she wasn't sure she only liked boys, they'd supported her and told her she didn't have to figure out any sort of label. If she did one day, great. If not, she should just be herself. Then, they'd met Ruby and come home raving about this young woman who'd started a Pride event in some small town about an hour away.

"Dad?" she said.

"Yes?" he replied, sitting down next to her on the bed.

"You know Ruby?"

"Of course."

"Well, we're going out tonight," she said hesitantly.

"You're hanging out with Ruby? Working on the festival?"

"No." Jaden laughed a little. "She's obsessed with that thing. I've convinced her to take the night off, though."

He looked at her confused as if Ruby only existed to work on this festival.

"Dad, we're *going* out."

"Where?"

"To the movies."

"Okay. Well, if you're going to be any later than midnight, call–"

"Dad, it's a date," she interrupted.

"A date?" he asked, catching up. "Oh, a *date*." His eyes went wide. "Honey?" he yelled, and Jaden knew he wasn't talking to her.

"Yeah?" her other dad said as he arrived at the doorway.

"Jaden is going on a date with *Ruby*," he told him.

Her other father looked at Jaden, smiled, and then back to his husband.

"We were right," he said.

"Really? That's all you have to say? I have my first date with a girl in, like, an hour, can't figure out what to wear, how to do my hair, what kind of makeup to put on, and you two are–"

They both laughed loudly. Then, they helped her get ready for her first date with a girl. They'd picked out for her a green scoop-neck T-shirt and a sweater because the theater would likely be cold. She had only a few pairs of jeans because most of her life was spent in uniform, but her dad suggested a pair of dark ones, and they told her to keep things casual, so she'd worn some white sneakers. Her hair was pulled back because the humidity would make it frizz everywhere, and she opted for a little foundation and some pink lipstick with some mascara and no eye makeup. When the doorbell rang, Jaden stood from the sofa, and her fathers stood at the same time.

"Oh… No. You two, sit down."

"We've met the boys you brought home," her father argued.

"Dad, you have your phone in your hand. What are the odds you have the camera ready?" Jaden asked, walking toward the door, grabbing her purse as she went. "We'll be back by midnight. Please don't embarrass me."

They laughed, but they didn't sit down. Jaden took a deep breath and pulled open the door.

"Hi," she said softly when she took in Ruby, who was wearing a black pair of jeans and a white T-shirt with what looked like a black sports bra underneath.

Ruby had a pair of black boots on, and her hair had some product in it for the first time that Jaden had seen. It was pushed back a little and made Ruby look a little like she belonged on a motorcycle.

"Hi," Ruby greeted. "I got you this." She held out a single white rose.

"You brought a flower?" Jaden's dad said from behind her.

Jaden rolled her eyes as she took the rose.

"Dad!"

Ruby smiled at her and said, "Should we go, or do I need to…" She pointed to Jaden's dads.

"No, they're annoying." Jaden turned back just in time to see her father take what was most likely, an awful picture of the two of them. "Dad!"

Ruby laughed, which made Jaden laugh, and she made her way onto the concrete slab that was their front porch, closing the door behind herself.

"Sorry about them. God, they're embarrassing. I'm eighteen years old," she said.

"They're sweet," Ruby replied.

"Well, next time, I'm picking *you* up, so you can be embarrassed by your own parents."

"Next time?" Ruby asked, looking hopeful as they walked the two steps that led to the driveway.

"Oh, I guess I just said that, huh?"

"I'm good with it," Ruby replied, unlocking her car with her fob.

She walked around to Jaden's side of the car and actually opened her door, smiling as Jaden slid into the seat. None of the guys Jaden had gone out with had ever opened a door for her, to her fathers' constant disappointment. Ruby closed it once Jaden was settled, and a few minutes later, they pulled up to the movie theater, where Ruby got them their tickets. When they went into the concession line to get some popcorn to share and a couple of drinks, Ruby insisted on paying again, even though Jaden had offered.

They moved inside the theater then, with Ruby holding their drinks and Jaden carrying the way-too-big popcorn container, smelling of fake butter and a little of chocolate, for some reason. Finding seats in the back, they sat down and organized their items. The popcorn was in Jaden's lap, and after talking for a few moments, Ruby dipped her hand inside and took a handful.

Thirty minutes later, the popcorn box was half-empty and sitting in the chair next to Jaden. Forty minutes later, Jaden felt something on her leg. She looked down and noticed Ruby's hand there, just resting. A few minutes after that, Jaden worked up enough courage to put her clammy hand on top of Ruby's. Ruby turned hers over, and their fingers entwined. An hour in, Jaden was laughing at the film with her head on Ruby's shoulder. Just before it was over, she felt Ruby's nose moving through her hair and then lips pressing to the top of her head. Jaden smiled and moved her face into Ruby's neck, closing her eyes and keeping it there until the movie was over, not caring about the ending anymore.

They held hands as they left the theater, and there was a funny moment where they'd attempted to throw their trash in the can but didn't want to let go of each other, either. Jaden's nearly finished drink almost crashed to the already sticky floor, but Ruby caught it for her, and they laughed at how ridiculous they were being.

Deciding on a walk after the movie, Jaden left her sweater in Ruby's car, and they walked through the small town of Monroe, ending up in a used bookstore just as it was about to close. They didn't buy anything but walked around and talked about their favorite books and hobbies.

Eventually, they got to the topic of majors, schools, and

life plans. It seemed so strange to Jaden that when she'd been sixteen, her main concern had been the school dance and who might ask her or what to wear on the out-of-uniform days at school. Then, a year later, she was worrying about college acceptances and SATs. Now, at eighteen, she was meant to have much of her life figured out.

"It's just a lot. I still feel like a kid. I have a curfew, you know?" she said when they arrived back at the house around eleven-thirty.

"Yeah, I get it," Ruby replied. "I don't know that I have *anything* figured out. I got into school, and that's good, but I don't know that you can really know what you'll do with the rest of your life when you're eighteen. I don't want to box myself into something I end up hating."

"Me neither," Jaden said.

Then, there was a moment of silence where they both stared at the red front door of Jaden's house.

"So," Ruby began. "Earlier, you said *next time.*"

"I did."

"Do you want there–"

"Yes," she interrupted.

Ruby laughed a little and said, "Me too. Come on. I'll walk you to the door. I don't want you to be late."

"I have thirty minutes," Jaden said, turning to her.

Ruby smiled at her for a long moment as if considering Jaden's meaning with that sentence.

"Ruby, I have thirty minutes," she repeated.

"You want to make out in this car right now?" Ruby asked, lifting an eyebrow.

"Yes." Jaden laughed, covering her face with both hands. "Was I not obvious enough?"

"I want to kiss you, Jade."

Jaden removed her hands then and looked at Ruby, concerned by her tone.

"But..."

"Your dads are pretending they're not watching us, but they're in the front window."

Jaden turned to see both of her fathers standing at the window. One was pretending to look at his phone, and the other was pretending to look away.

"Oh, I'll kill them."

Ruby laughed and said, "Next time?"

"Fine," she said, irritated.

"I'll walk you to the door."

"You don't have to do that," Jaden said.

"No, I should. They're watching, and I want them to let you go out with me again. Stay there."

Ruby got out of the car, walked around, and opened the door for Jaden. They walked hand in hand to the front stoop and turned toward one another, standing there awkwardly for another minute before Ruby dragged her feet a bit, moving them closer together.

"So, I know you can't date during the week, but next weekend is good?"

"Yeah," Jaden replied. "Whenever." She shuffled her feet until they were standing as close together as they could get.

Ruby pressed her forehead to Jaden's. Jaden gasped and thought this was it. This was going to be her first kiss with another girl, and it would be with Ruby. Instead, Ruby kissed her cheek, pressed their foreheads back together, and bit her lower lip.

"I cannot believe you two," Jaden said loudly toward her fathers when she entered the house.

CHAPTER 7

Jo wasn't paying attention to whatever the principal was saying. It was an afternoon assembly with the entire school present. The freshmen were on the left side of the bleachers with the sophomores. The juniors were on the right side with the seniors, and the principal was standing on the gym floor, holding on to a microphone, with a few teachers around him talking about final exams, clearing out lockers, and other end-of-year items. Jo knew she'd regret not paying attention later, but she couldn't stop staring over at Chance, who was sitting next to Ruby and whispering something to her. Jo smiled, wishing she had a best friend the way they had each other.

Chance was smiling and appeared to be happy, and that made Jo happy. She just wished she would've been the one making Chance laugh right now. Instead, she rolled her eyes internally at herself and turned her head back to the principal who was going on about rented textbooks and how to turn them back in at the library once they were finished with classes.

"Hey," someone said.

Jo turned to the girl sitting next to her and offered her a shy smile.

"Hi," she said, not believing that someone was actually talking to her.

"Can we go?" the girl asked, pointing toward the end of the bleachers.

It was then that Jo noticed that students had stood and were walking down the bleachers toward the doors.

"Oh, sorry." She stood up, walked quickly to the aisle, and headed down until she was on the gym floor, looking up and over to find Chance and Ruby.

They were walking out of the gym together, though, and Jo wouldn't be able to catch up in time before the next period. She hadn't made any other friends yet. She'd been sitting next to Chance and Ruby at lunch most days, and they were great, but Jo had tried talking to a few kids in her various classes and the girl with the locker next to hers. They'd been polite enough, but despite her best efforts, she'd yet to make a connection with anyone other than Chance. Ruby was nice, but every free second she had was spent texting with Jaden. Chance didn't have a boyfriend, which meant she had time for Jo.

"Hey, need a ride?" Chance asked at the end of the school day.

"How did you know?" Jo asked, closing her locker.

"You've been parking next to me, and I didn't see your car when I went outside for gym."

"It's worse than just the battery, and we don't have the money to fix it, so I've been taking the bus or walking."

"Jo, why didn't you tell me?" Chance asked as they walked down the crowded hallway. "I can pick you up and take you home."

"That's not fair to you. I couldn't even pay you gas money because I don't have a job yet, and we need the money to actually fix my car."

"You don't have to pay me," Chance replied. "I like hanging out with you. Driving you home is just a hangout session." She smiled over at Jo. "Anyway, I'm going to the community center. Ruby asked me to meet her there because the LGBTQ+ center from Greenfield is sending two people tonight to talk about the booths they'll have there. Ruby wanted some help, I guess."

"I can go with you," Jo offered.

"Yeah, that's the idea. Save me from third wheel hell." She slipped her arm through Jo's, adding, "Jaden will be there."

Jo laughed as they headed outside toward Chance's car. Not long after, they arrived at the community center, spotting Ruby standing in front of a car, with Jaden between her and the vehicle. They weren't touching exactly, but they were standing very closely together, and they were both smiling like idiots at each other, which probably meant they were in love or well on their way to that.

"Hey, hands to yourself. I don't want to see that," Chance said.

"We weren't even doing anything," Ruby replied, laughing. "You two have met, right?" she asked Jo of Jaden.

"Yeah, hi," Jo said.

"Hey," Jaden replied.

"I thought you couldn't do anything on the weekdays," Chance noted.

"My dads are inside. They're the ones in charge of coordinating the booths, and I'm just tagging along so I can see this one." Jaden reached out and touched Ruby's T-shirt.

"You look cute in your uniform," Ruby told her.

"Shut up." Jaden laughed.

"Where should we go?" Chance asked.

"Inside. I'll be right in," Ruby said.

"They want to make out," Chance whispered to Jo, taking Jo's hand and entwining their fingers.

Jo looked down at their linked hands, smiled, and looked quickly back up. Ruby lifted an eyebrow at her, and Jo wiped the smile from her face. Ruby gave her an expression that showed her pity and returned her attention to Jaden.

Jo allowed herself to be pulled inside the building and into the room where she saw Jaden's dads talking to two women and another man in the corner. Jo didn't know exactly what was needed of her, so she just kept herself connected to Chance as much as possible for over an hour until the booth ideas were locked down, the shifts were set for people to man them, and the people from the center needed to hit the road to get home.

"Want to go to *Carver's*?" Ruby asked.

"Sure," Chance said. "Jo?"

"Um… yeah. Ice cream?"

"They have hot dogs and corn dogs, too. Sometimes, hamburgers. It just depends on what they order each week," Chance explained.

"Oh, yeah. I'm starving," she replied.

"Jaden?" Chance asked Ruby.

"She has to go. Her dads drove her here," Ruby said, sounding disappointed.

"Well, let's drown your sorrows in a milkshake," Chance suggested, wrapping her arm around Ruby's shoulders. "I'm buying."

They drove in Ruby's car, leaving Chance's at the center for now, and found *Carver's* to be busy. Waiting in line for a few minutes, Jo was finally able to order a chili dog at Chance's insistence. Chance got one as well, and Ruby stuck with a corn dog with mustard. They all got milkshakes and shared a large container of French fries in the middle of the table. Jo listened to Ruby and Chance talk about Jaden for a long while as she ate her dinner.

"She's so..." Ruby said, looking skyward. "God, Chance, I've never felt like this before."

"You're eighteen; it's not like we've lived all that long to have felt much of anything," Chance argued.

"Yeah, but she's..."

"Going to ever finish that sentence?" she teased.

"She's amazing, and I'm totally crazy about her. I just want to talk to her all the time, and I hated that I had to say goodbye to her back there."

"Okay. Calm down. You just met the girl," Chance reasoned.

"I don't think it works like that," Jo said, surprising herself.

"Huh?" Chance turned to her.

"Oh," Jo said, realizing the attention was on her now. "Just that you can't help how you feel, right? You like someone. It happens. Hopefully, they like you back."

"I guess so, yeah," Chance replied, smiling warmly at her. "So, you've felt this before, then?" Chance asked her.

Jo looked over at Ruby, silently asking her for help.

"Anyway, Jade is amazing. That's all I'm saying. We're going out again, and I can't wait."

Jo looked at her thankfully. They finished eating, tossed

their trash, and hopped back into Ruby's car. After driving back to pick up Chance's car, Ruby used the Bluetooth in her own to connect instantly to Jaden, who had just gotten home, and Jo overheard them talking as Ruby drove out of the lot with her windows rolled down.

"Do you not like Jaden?" Jo asked once they were inside Chance's car.

"What? No, I like her. Why?"

"You were kind of talking Ruby out of her feelings a little back there."

"I wasn't. I just worry about her. She's starting her first real relationship right when we're about to leave, and Jaden is going to school six hours away from where we'll be. I just don't want her to get her heart broken."

"What about you?"

"Me?" Chance asked.

"Yeah. Do you have anyone special you'll miss like that when you leave?"

They pulled up to a red light.

"Hey, what did you think about the whole Pride parade thing they mentioned earlier?" Chance asked instead, deftly changing the subject.

"The people from the center?"

"Yeah."

"I guess it's a cool idea. I'd like to help with it. Maybe I can be more involved next year than I am this year."

"You'd *have* to be," Chance said. "Ruby and I won't be here."

Jo watched Chance for a moment longer before turning her head and staring out the window instead. Jo's only friends would be moving away in a few months, and the girl Jo liked more than anyone ever before was one of those friends.

CHAPTER 8

"When is she getting here?" Chance asked.

"In ten minutes. How do I look?" Ruby asked, turning around in place.

"You've never asked me that before while getting ready for a date," Chance noted.

"Because I've had so many of those," Ruby said sarcastically. "Come on, Chance. How do I look?"

"Fine," Chance said, shrugging.

"I hate you," Ruby replied, chuckling.

"What do you want me to say? You look good, I guess."

Ruby was wearing a black T-shirt with her faux-leather jacket over it that made her feel like a badass. Her gray jeans were skinny at the ankles and disappeared under her black motorcycle boots.

"Chance, it's our second date."

"I know that," Chance replied. "I also know you're totally insane over this girl."

"We talk every day," she said wistfully.

"Trust me, we know," Chance replied.

"We?" Ruby asked, grabbing her phone and wallet and tucking them into her back pockets.

"Yeah."

"Who's the *we*, Chance?"

"Oh. Jo, obviously," Chance replied as if it were evident.

And it *was* obvious to Ruby, but she wanted Chance to say it. Chance and Jo had been spending a lot of time together since they'd met, and Ruby already knew that Jo had at least a crush on Chance, so she wondered if the reason Chance was hanging out with Jo so much was that Ruby had been so busy with Jaden, but she'd also seen her with Jo, and there was something there. She wouldn't force her best friend to admit something she wasn't ready to or she wouldn't do anything about. While true that Chance believed human sexuality was fluid, she'd never said anything to Ruby about being interested in girls or anyone other than the one or two boys in their school that she'd dated over the years.

"You like Jo, huh?" Ruby asked softly, thinking that was a safe question to ask.

"Yeah, she's cool. I've been picking her up and dropping her off because her car sucks, and we've been hanging out, too."

"I know I've been busy with Jaden and the festival, and it's probably shit timing since we're about to graduate and every-thing…"

Chance laughed and stood.

"What?"

"Ruby, maybe it would be like that if I were going to school in California and you were going somewhere in, like, Florida, but we're literally living together next year. It's not like we're leaving each other; just leaving home. Have fun with Jaden while you can."

"Fun?"

"Yeah, fun," she said.

"It's not *just* fun, Chance."

"I know, but she's going to be over six hours away."

"So? We can figure that part out." Ruby shrugged as they began walking out of her bedroom.

"I'm sure you can. I just don't want you to get hurt, Ruby."

"I know, and thanks. But Jade is like no one I've ever met, and I know it's only a second date, but it just feels… different. It feels kind of epic, Chance."

"Epic?" Chance said with a teasing smile.

"Yes, epic. I said what I said. Now, get out of here. She'll be here soon."

Chance laughed and made her way to the front door once they were downstairs. She opened the door, turned back around, and gave Ruby a once-over.

"You look great, Ruby. Have a good date, okay?"

"Thanks." Ruby smiled as her friend left.

***

Ruby's parents had gone out to dinner themselves, so she was alone as she paced in her living room. Jaden had offered to drive to Ruby's tonight instead of Ruby going to Monroe to get her, but that meant that they'd be stuck in this much smaller town, and since it was a date, that left Ruby wondering what they could possibly do. Her parents had told her that it would be fine to have Jaden over to watch a movie while they were out, but Ruby wanted something more than sitting on the couch, holding hands while a movie played, until her parents got home and interrupted their date.

When the doorbell rang, she grabbed the bag she'd packed and pulled the door open quickly, unable to hide her excitement at seeing Jaden again and being able to go out with her tonight. Jaden herself was smiling wide as if she was having the same problem. She was wearing a pair of jeans and a blue sweater with the Adidas logo on the front of it in white. She looked perfectly casual, and even though Ruby's eyes went to Jaden's breasts, which looked good in that sweater, and she wanted to take the thing off of Jaden and explore Jaden's body, she managed to clear her throat and meet Jaden's eyes quickly, hoping Jaden hadn't noticed.

"Big Adidas fan?" Jaden said, smirking at Ruby.

"Yes, *big* fan," Ruby replied, choosing to admit it.

Jaden laughed and said, "Are you ready?"

"Yeah." She held up the bag.

"Why do you have a bag?"

"Oh, we're going somewhere."

"Somewhere that requires a bag?"

"Just shut up." Ruby laughed, left the house, locked the door behind her, and took Jaden's hand. "You look great, by the way."

"I know. I caught you staring at my *sweater*," Jaden teased.

"Well, it's a great sweater."

The house was on the lake, but Ruby didn't want to sit outside her house because her parents would probably notice them and that Ruby's car was still there, and they'd approach and interrupt, so they drove her car around the lake a bit to an inlet that was hidden by the trees and had a small gravel beach, if one could call it that. Most of the town knew about the big parts of the lake where everyone gathered, but this inlet wasn't as popular or well-known. Chance and Ruby had discovered it themselves only a few years ago when they'd walked the creek and then kept going until they spotted a thick grouping of trees and a family of rabbits running. They followed, giving the animals space, and ended up at the inlet.

"Wow! This is nice, Ruby," Jaden said, looking out at the lake.

"Yeah. I thought we could just hang here tonight. It's not too hot, and I brought this bug thing to put next to the blanket to keep them away."

"Bugs?" Jaden said, turning back to her.

"I'll protect you," she teased.

A few minutes later, Ruby had a blanket on the pebbles and everything else set up. The sun was still up, but it wouldn't be for long, and she'd turn the bug thing on then to help keep them out of their space. She'd brought a few snacks and some drinks, but other than her phone, which she turned on to a Spotify playlist and had working softly in the background, the only sounds were of nature around them.

"This is nice," Jaden said.

"Yeah, it is," Ruby replied.

She lifted a second blanket and moved it over Jaden's shoulders. Then, she leaned back on her hands and stared out over the water.

"I'm kind of totally into you," Jaden admitted several minutes into the silence.

Ruby turned to her and said, "Well, I'm kind of totally into you."

"So, it works out, then," Jaden joked, nodding.

"Yeah, I guess."

"Ruby?"

"Yeah?"

"Do you maybe want to lie down?"

Ruby swallowed and nodded slowly. Jaden moved the blanket around herself and held it out for Ruby to take, too. They both moved until they were lying flat on the ground, staring up at the clear sky that was fading from the bright blue of the day and into the pinks and oranges of dusk. Neither of them said anything. Ruby reached for Jaden's hand and took it under the blanket that was now on top of them, even though it wasn't yet cold enough to need it.

Several minutes later, Jaden turned onto her side, facing Ruby. Ruby turned her head at first, but realizing Jaden was staring at her, she turned her whole body, disconnecting their hands in the process. She stared into Jaden's mesmerizing eyes and could tell they were smiling back at her. Ruby cupped Jaden's cheek, needing to touch her somehow, and Jaden moved closer to her. Ruby moved a little closer, too, until they were nearly pressed together. Jaden's arm went around Ruby's waist and stilled there.

"I want to kiss you," Ruby told her, licking her lips as if it were about to happen, but she'd wait for Jaden to tell her that it was okay first.

"Yeah, okay," Jaden replied.

"Are you sure? We don't—"

"I'm sure," Jaden said, smiling softly.

Ruby leaned in, pressing their foreheads together first to give Jaden an out, but Jaden didn't take it, so she connected their lips hesitantly at first, pulling back a few millimeters and staring into Jaden's eyes again. They were still smiling, so she leaned back in and didn't pull away this time. It was Jaden who deepened the kiss, and Ruby moved her arm around Jaden's waist, needing her to be as close as possible while they did this. Ruby wasn't sure how long they kissed like that before her tongue slipped into Jaden's mouth, and Jaden gave the tiniest of moans back. Ruby wanted to move on top of her then, but this was their first kiss, and Jaden hadn't ever kissed a girl before, so Ruby slowed the kiss and waited until Jaden pulled back.

"Can we do that again?" Jaden asked, looking a little dazed.

"Yes," Ruby said, chuckling at her.

"Like, now?"

Ruby leaned back in and kissed her again.

CHAPTER 9

Jaden drove home after hours at the lake with Ruby. It had been a perfect second date, and she was looking forward to their third. Because she could only date on the weekends, they'd arranged for it to be Saturday night after their Friday night date. Jaden was already in town for the festival preparations, so they decided to hit up the lake again and make that their special spot. Before they could get to the date, though, they had some work to do.

"The tents won't be delivered until, like, right before," Ruby said.

"Is that enough time?" Jo asked her.

"Yeah, the company puts them up for us, so they know what they're doing," Ruby replied.

The four of them had taken a break from their work and had sat outside the community center on the steps, drinking water and having a quick snack before they got back to work. Jaden was sitting next to Ruby, who was ever the leader, and damn, it was kind of a turn-on. Ruby ran a hand through her hair, pushing it away from her face, and Jaden wanted to reach over and do it again just because.

Ruby smiled at her as Chance asked something of Jo, and Jaden decided to just go for it. She reached out and ran her hand through that short hair, loving the feel of it as her fingers moved through it. She'd done this last night, too, as they'd made out under the trees by the water. She'd wanted Ruby to move on top of her and take the lead, but Ruby had kept things pretty PG last night, to Jaden's disappointment. It wasn't *all* that disappointing, though. Ruby's soft lips were amazing, and Jaden was ready to have them on her own lips again. She wasn't ready to take things all the way with Ruby just yet, but she knew she wanted a little more than what they'd had last night.

"What are you two up to tonight?" Chance asked.

"Date night," Jaden replied, taking Ruby's hand in her own. "I'm kind of obsessed with her, I think."

"Obsessed, huh?" Ruby teased, looking at her with those big brown eyes.

"What about you two?" Jaden asked to be polite.

"Us?" Chance asked, turning to Jo. "What are *we* doing tonight?"

"Oh," Jo said, looking a little confused. "I don't know. Did you want to do something?"

"You can't have the inlet," Ruby said. "That's ours tonight."

Chance laughed and said, "Fine. Whatever. Want to watch a movie at my place?" she asked Jo.

"Sure," Jo replied, smiling a little.

Jaden looked at Ruby and smiled at her, nodding toward the other two.

"So, we're watching a movie, apparently," Chance told them.

***

Several hours later, the work was done for the day. Jaden felt sweaty and dirty, but Ruby told her she looked great, and Jaden believed her. Ruby had this way of making her feel like she was the only person in the room, even when they were surrounded by people. They stopped by *Carver's* and picked up food to-go, arriving at the lake with the blanket shortly after. They ate in relative silence, sharing fries and trying each other's ice cream. The kissing started shortly after, and when Ruby moved to lie down, Jaden went with her.

Jaden wasn't sure how long they lay there exchanging slow kisses, but after a while, she moved to lie against Ruby's chest. She slipped her hand under Ruby's shirt and rested it against her stomach, loving that she could touch Ruby like this.

"It's weird," she admitted after a moment.

"What is?" Ruby asked.

"You're the first girl I've ever kissed."

"And that's *weird*?" Ruby chuckled.

Jaden could feel it against her own body, and she loved it.

"It's weird that I like it so much. I didn't really know, I guess. Then, there was you… And now, I'm totally into you."

"I'm totally into you, too," Ruby said.

"Can I ask you something?"

"Sure."

"Well, you know you're the only girl I've ever kissed…"

"Oh," Ruby said, realizing where this conversation was going.

"But you've done more than just kissing, right?" Jaden asked.

"You really want to know?"

"Yes," Jaden said.

Ruby sighed and said, "Yeah, I've done that before."

"With a girl?"

"*Only* with girls."

"So, it was more than one?"

"No, I just meant that I've never been with a guy – never wanted to be with a guy."

"So, one girl?"

"Yes."

"When?"

"I was fifteen."

"Fifteen? Wow."

"Is that bad?" Ruby asked, wrapping her arm around Jaden more tightly.

"No, I just walked around the mall a bunch at fifteen; I wasn't thinking about having sex."

Ruby chuckled and said, "It was a spur of the moment the first time."

"The *first* time? How many times were there?"

"A few."

"How many is a few?" Jaden asked, laughing.

"Jade, do you really want details?" she said, sounding a little irritated.

"No details."

"It was a summer camp thing. Chance and I were counselors for the summer. I met someone there, and she and I were both into girls. We had a brief relationship, and yeah, we had sex a few times, but it was mainly because neither of us had ever done that, and it ended before we left."

Jaden sat up then and stared out at the water.

"Jade, I'm sorry."

"What? Why?" Jaden asked, turning back to her.

"I don't know. You seem upset now."

"I'm not upset," she said. "I was just thinking that I wish I would've known you then."

"Yeah? Why?" Ruby asked, sitting up as well and leaning back on her hands.

"Because maybe *I* could have been your first," she replied, smiling back at her.

"You want that?"

"Not today, but yeah."

Ruby smiled at her and replied, "I wish I would've waited, then."

"Was it any good, at least?" Jaden teased.

"What?" Ruby laughed.

"Did she... you know... get you there?"

"Jade!"

Jaden moved into her then, forcing Ruby to lie back down as Jaden climbed on top of her.

"What? I want to know."

"Yeah, she did. Well, once."

"Only once?" Jaden asked, connecting their foreheads together.

"Yes, only once. Neither of us knew what we were doing."

"Did she use her hands or her mouth?"

"Oh, my God!" Ruby blushed, and it was adorable.

"Tell me, or I'll tickle you."

Ruby laughed as Jaden's hand moved back under her shirt and rested on her side.

"Hands. Well, fingers; she wasn't ready for the other thing."

"So, no one's ever…"

"No. Now, can we talk about something else, please?"

Jaden pressed their lips together and deepened the kiss as Ruby's arms wrapped firmly around her.

"I want to be the only one you do this with," Jaden said, moving her lips to Ruby's neck. "Can we be together?"

"You want to be my girlfriend?" Ruby asked, letting out a little whimper as Jaden moved her lips over her collarbone.

"Yes."

"Okay," Ruby replied.

Jaden looked down at Ruby's shirt, which had gotten a little bunched, and met Ruby's eyes after.

"Can I just…" She slid her hand a little higher.

"What?" Ruby asked.

"See you a little?"

"See me?" Her face showed recognition. "You want me to… take off my shirt?"

"I just want to touch you here." She placed a tentative hand over Ruby's bra-covered breast.

"Oh," Ruby said.

"Wow," Jaden replied when she felt a nipple harden beneath her hand. "Really?"

"Yeah, really," Ruby replied.

Jaden lifted Ruby's shirt and stared down at her own hand on Ruby's breast.

"It's okay. You can touch me."

Jaden squeezed the breast a little and watched as Ruby's eyes closed. She lowered her head and rested it between Ruby's breasts, breathing in. Then, she kissed the spot before she moved her lips to Ruby's other breast, seeing the nipple pressing into the fabric. She lowered her lips to it, kissing it once.

"God," Ruby let out.

"Okay?"

"Yes," Ruby said.

"Can I see–"

"Yes," Ruby interrupted.

She sat up a little and removed her shirt, causing Jaden to

bite her lip as she watched Ruby pull off her sports bra and lie back down on the blanket. The way Ruby did that showed her confidence, and Jaden found that confidence to be so sexy. Jaden lowered herself back on top of her and kissed Ruby's lips, knowing that in just a minute, she'd lower her own to Ruby's breasts.

"Jade, you don't–"

Jaden silenced her with a kiss before she moved her lips back to Ruby's neck.

"I want to. Just this tonight, okay?"

"Can I see you at least?"

"Maybe," she teased. "You're so beautiful, Ruby." She lowered her lips to Ruby's chest.

"You're going to get me going and leave me hanging, aren't you?" Ruby laughed.

"You're not going yet?" Jaden teased more, hovering her lips over Ruby's nipple.

"No, I'm definitely going." She gasped when Jaden kissed her nipple hesitantly. "Jesus!"

Jaden smiled and repeated the movement a few more times until Ruby's hand was in her hair, giving her a not-so-subtle push downward. Jaden sucked on her nipple then and earned another of those addictive gasps.

CHAPTER 10

"That was a little intimidating," Jo said.

"Why?" Chance asked as they walked down the steps.

"There were, like, ten cops in there."

"It *is* a police station." Chance laughed.

"I know, but I've never been around that many cops before."

"I guess that means you've never been arrested, so that's a good thing."

"You're hilarious," Jo said sarcastically, running a hand into that messy hair. "I was sweating."

"Why? We were just asking for volunteers for festival security."

"I don't know. I worried they might ask me about a speeding ticket I got back home that I might not have ever paid."

"You're *such* a daredevil," Chance joked.

"Well, I'm no Ruby with her motorcycle boots and badass leather jacket."

"It's not real leather, and Ruby's never been on a motorcycle in her life. She just likes the look."

"Well, it works for her."

"She's taken, Jo," Chance teased as they arrived at her car, and she unlocked it.

"What? I'm not, like, into her. I just meant that she has a look. That's cool."

"Do *I* have a look?" Chance asked, getting behind the wheel.

"I'd call your look casual preppy."

"What?" She laughed as she put the key in the ignition.

"Yeah, you're like… casual, but preppy."

"I'm preppy?"

"Not in a bad way. It works for you." Jo shrugged a shoulder.

"What's *your* look, then?"

"Slob?" Jo said.

"Shut up. You aren't a slob," Chance argued.

"What am I, then?"

"Cute," Chance replied without thinking.

"I'm cute?" Jo said, turning to her.

Chance pulled out of the parking lot, trying to stall having to answer that question and feeling the blush creep on her cheeks.

"You're in cute tennis shoes a lot that have those scuff marks on them, and your jeans have holes at the knees sometimes. I don't know; it's cute."

"That's just called *poor*, Chance."

Chance didn't know what to say to that.

"Well, I like it," she finally replied. "And I like your old band shirts, and how sometimes you have the shirt tucked into your jeans in the front, but not the sides or the back."

"I didn't know you noticed that."

"Yeah, I notice things," Chance said.

"Right," Jo replied.

"Anyway… Ready to wash some cars now to make some money?"

"I guess."

Now that they had the police department locked down to volunteer for the festival, they'd helped in the budget overage department a little, but the food still cost a lot to get, and until the festival was over and they could count the profit, they had to pay the bills, as Ruby had said, so there would be a few events prior to the festival where they tried to make some money to host the thing, to begin with. Chance had worn her bathing suit under her clothes for their trip to the police station, and Jo had worn a pair of red-and-blue board shorts and appeared to have a sports bra on under her T-shirt.

When they got there, Ruby was already in full command, telling everyone where to go and what to do. Chance was put on hose duty; Jo was wiping down cars. Jaden was collecting money, and Ruby was still playing the director's role an hour later as cars began really piling up. They needed at least a hundred cars to make a thousand bucks, so this wouldn't be the event that truly helped with money, but it *would* bring more awareness to the festival itself, and Ruby had put the word out on social media far and wide to get people to come with their cars or just to hang out and buy some of the water and food they had on offer as well. Jaden had told her entire school, and she'd already seen a few people from *Monroe Prep* stop by.

The car wash was in full swing when Chance changed jobs with a girl from school and took over wiping down the next car. That was when she was promptly sprayed with the hose.

"Jo!" Chance held her hands up, trying to keep the spray from her face while Jo cackled with laughter.

"You looked hot." Jo sprayed her again.

Chance laughed and looked down at herself. She was wearing a pair of shorts and just her blue-and-white bikini top now. Jo was still laughing.

"Not fair," she replied. "I didn't spray you when I was on hose duty."

"You're nicer than me, I guess."

"Well, obviously," Chance said. "Give me that thing; it's my turn."

"Oh, no way," Jo said, backing up.

Chance followed until she had Jo trapped between her body and the car. She looked down at the hose in Jo's hand, reaching for it and placing her own hand over Jo's. Jo just stood there, looking serious all of a sudden. Chance didn't know what to do. She knew if she tried to take the hose now, Jo would let her, but there was something in Jo's expression that told her that they weren't joking anymore.

"You're lucky it's hot out here," Chance said finally.

"*Yes*, I am," Jo said, swallowing.

"I like your board shorts, by the way."

"You do? They were on sale," Jo replied.

Chance looked down at them and said, "They look good on you. They suit you, somehow."

"Do they? I never know what to wear when swimsuits are involved."

"Why not?"

"I don't know. I don't really feel like I'm a bikini kind of person, but I can't go topless around people, either, and just rock board shorts."

"Do you want that?" Chance asked.

"Not really."

"Well, board shorts and sports bras are a good look. Ruby rocks that usually when there's a bathing suit involved. You could lose the T-shirt if you're hot, though." Chance pointed to the old band T that Jo was wearing over the sports bra.

"I'm okay. I mean, it's fine."

"Jo?"

"Yeah?"

"Just be yourself, okay? Whomever that is, it's pretty great."

"I don't know that I *know* who I am yet," Jo replied.

"Who does?" Chance said, smiling. "Now, I'm taking this hose because car wash rules say that if someone sprays you with water, you have to spray them back. It's like a whole thing."

"It is not." Jo laughed.

Chance stole the hose and sprayed, starting at Jo's head, wetting that messy hair first before she sprayed that shirt and those shorts. Jo laughed and chased her until the hose was out of Chance's hands.

"Hey!" Ruby yelled playfully.

Chance laughed as Jo dropped the hose. Then, she stopped when Jo pulled the shirt over and off and tossed it onto a lawn chair set up over by the food tables.

"Happy?" Jo said.

"Yeah," Chance replied, serious now as she lowered her eyes. "Sorry, what?"

"Nothing," Jo said, laughing still.

"Chance, can I borrow you?" Ruby asked.

"I'll be right back." Chance joined Ruby, who was by herself at one of the tables. "What's up? Jo sprayed me with that thing first. I was only–"

"It's not about that."

"Oh, okay. Well, if it's about how in love you are with Jaden, can I have a reprieve for one day? I know she, like, hangs the Moon or whatever you told me the other day in school, but–"

"You'd tell me, right?" Ruby interrupted.

"Tell you what?"

"If you were into someone," she said.

"Into someone?"

"Yeah, if you liked someone. You always tell me."

"Yes. Why?" Chance asked, instinctually turning to Jo.

"Yeah, that's what I thought."

"Huh?" Chance asked, turning back to Ruby.

"You know she's gay, Chance."

"Who?"

"Cut the crap," Ruby said, shaking her head. "Jo."

"Yes, I know that."

"Hey," Jaden said, walking up to them. "Sorry to interrupt. My phone's dead. Can I use yours to run the credit cards?" she asked Ruby.

"Sure." Ruby pulled it out of her back pocket and handed it to her.

"Unlock it for me?"

"I'll just give you the password."

"Oh, gross." Chance laughed. "I'm going back to work now. Let me know when you settle on a wedding date."

Jaden laughed, and Ruby just shook her head. Chance walked back over to the cars, where she saw Jo wiping the hood of one. Jo was bent over with the sponge, and despite only having on a sports bra and having small breasts, Chance got a decent view of the line between them. She licked her lips and stared. She actually stared at Jo's body.

It was true that Chance had always believed that human

sexuality was a complex thing that no one fully understood. Her mother was a therapist who had written a book on that very topic and had let Chance read it when she was fourteen after Ruby had come out to her. It had helped Chance understand that everyone was different – they loved who they loved and how they loved, and it was okay.

Chance hadn't considered herself perfectly straight after that because it seemed more likely to her that people were probably along that spectrum somewhere. She'd never been interested in any girls, though. She'd dated a few guys at school and hadn't ever had an attraction toward Ruby, who was her best friend in the world. She'd thought she might explore things a little when she got to college, but she didn't have plans to experiment or anything – she just wanted to be open-minded to the idea that the person who was meant for her might not look like the guys she'd dated. Her human would be her human, and that was all she'd care about.

Now, she was staring at Jo Hemsworth, the new kid in town, who was sweet and funny and who Chance loved hanging out with. She had spent more time with Jo than Ruby recently, and she'd never stared at Ruby how she was staring at Jo right now, thinking about how it might feel to hold Jo's breasts in her hands or kiss those full lips that seemed in a constant pout unless Jo was actively trying to smile.

"Hey, are you going to help or just stand there, Curtis?" Jo yelled at her and threw the sponge in Chance's direction.

CHAPTER 11

"I wish this was all just done already," Ruby said, staring down at her phone.

"School? Lunch?" Chance asked.

"School. I want summer to be here already."

"She knows that when summer hits, Jaden can hang out whenever she wants because her dads will drop that weeknight rule thing," Chance told Jo.

Jo hadn't been all that focused on whatever Ruby had been saying. Jo had waited for Chance in the cafeteria, holding her place in line like she usually did because Jo's locker was closer to the cafeteria, and Jo got here before Chance did every day.

"Oh," Jo said.

Chance sat down with her tray and asked, "You okay there?"

"Yeah. Why?"

"I don't know. You just seem like you're zoned out."

"Who's zoned out?" Ruby asked, sitting down across from Chance.

"Me," Jo replied, sitting down next to Chance, like always.

"Oh. What's up?" Ruby asked.

"I'm just tired."

Ruby looked down at her phone as a message must have come in. The phone was on silent since they weren't strictly allowed to be used on campus, but the school seemed pretty lax in dealing with it.

"Sorry, it's Jaden," Ruby said. "I'm thinking of doing something at the house for Memorial Day."

"A party?" Chance asked her.

"No, just like a few people."

"So, Jaden?" Chance joked.

"I can't just have *her* over. My parents will be gone, and they're cool, but I don't think they want my girlfriend to stay the weekend with me. Besides, her dads wouldn't allow that anyway."

"Why? You're both eighteen," Jo said.

"Still kids in the eyes of our parents, though," Ruby reasoned. "Anyway, I was thinking about just the four of us."

"The four of us?" Jo asked.

"Yeah, me and Jaden, and you two. We can do an end-of-the-school-year sleepover or something."

"Your parents will allow Jaden to sleep over?" Jo asked her.

"We'll figure that part out later," Ruby said, typing a response to Jaden.

"Hey, want to eat outside?" Chance asked.

"Me?" Jo asked back when she noticed Chance wasn't looking at Ruby anymore.

"Yeah, *you*. That one is too busy to take lunch outside," she said, pointing to Ruby.

"I heard that. But yeah, I'm good here."

"I can't – I'm a junior; only seniors can eat outside."

"No one pays attention. Come on," Chance said, standing up with her tray.

"Okay. But if I get in trouble, I'm telling them it was peer pressure." Jo stood.

"So, why are you so tired?" Chance asked when they sat down on the school's front stairs with their trays sitting on the ground next to them.

"I've just been helping my mom out at home more. When we first got here, she gave me a reprieve to get caught up at school and make friends, but she works a lot, so I need to help around the house when I can. Laundry, vacuuming, cooking dinner, dishes, and stuff like that. I was going to get a part-time job, but she told me to wait until the summer to do that since it's so close to the end of the year."

"Where are you going to work?" Chance asked.

"No idea," Jo replied. "I went online to see if anything was posted on the school job board, but there wasn't anything I could really see myself doing. There was someone who wanted a part-time landscaper."

"So, someone to mow lawns?"

"Yeah, and I can do that, but–"

"You melted in our April heat, so how will you deal with the summer heat while pushing a lawn mower?" Chance teased.

Jo laughed and said, "Exactly. I'll find something, though."

Chance had this thing where she could finish Ruby's sentences, and Ruby had it with Chance, too, but Jo hadn't had that with anyone in her life. Now, Jo noticed Chance was starting to do it – finishing Jo's sentences, knowing what Jo was going to say or what Jo was thinking – and it was nice. Jo looked at her then as Chance was staring across the small patch of grass that the school called a quad and toward the football field.

"It's so weird. Soon, I'll be sitting in a chair on that field, wearing a cap and gown and graduating from this place."

"Are you going to miss it?" Jo asked.

"High school? No. But yeah, this place. As much as I want to leave and go to college, this place was six years of my life. When I got here, Ruby and I were scrawny seventh-graders who couldn't believe we had to go to school with the seniors who looked so much older and cooler than we felt. Now, we *are* those seniors, and it's almost over. I've walked the same hallways for years, knowing where all my classes are even before the first day of school because nothing ever changes here. I guess I'm a little nervous about school. I don't know the campus well, and I won't know anyone other than Ruby. Classes change every semester, and I'll have to relearn where they are. It's a lot, you know?"

"Yeah, but at least you'll have Ruby. That's good, right?"

"We'll see. I know she's my best friend, but she's a little hooked on love right now, and I don't see that dying down when we move into our apartment. I think she and Jaden will go crazy being all over each other this summer and try to make it work when we all go to college. I leave in July, so Ruby will only have Jaden – which is good: I want her to have someone, and I love that she's happy – but when I'll get to school with her, I just see her being on the phone with Jaden constantly, and me having to listen to them tell each other how in love they are, and how they'll make this work. Jaden will visit, and I'll be wearing noise-canceling headphones all weekend. I hope this part doesn't happen, but if they can't make it, and they break up because it's too hard, I'll have to console my best friend and her broken heart. It's not something I thought we'd need to deal with right away. I thought we'd both get there, settle in, and then maybe find people, you know?"

"Noise-canceling headphones? Really?" Jo teased, trying to lighten Chance's serious tone.

"I don't know if they'll be loud or not, but I don't want to hear it either way."

"They've already had sex?"

"Not yet, but they will."

"Oh. Yeah. I mean, I guess that makes sense."

Chance turned and said, "Makes sense that they'd have sex? They're together."

"Well, when you're not with anyone, that's not always something you're thinking about happening... I know it happens, obviously; I just wasn't thinking they were there yet – it hasn't been that long."

"They haven't yet, so I guess they're not there, but they will be. Ruby says Jaden's into the idea of it, and with the inevitability of us all leaving soon, I'm sure it'll happen this summer."

"I wouldn't want that."

"Sex?" Chance asked, smiling at Jo.

"No, I want sex," Jo replied.

There was the sound of laughter coming from behind them, and Jo turned to see that two other seniors had overheard their conversation and were now laughing.

"Goodbye, Alicia. Bye, Steph," Chance said.

Jo turned back to see Chance glaring at them.

"Sorry. Back to you," Chance said to Jo.

"I just meant that I've never... so... when I do, I wouldn't want it to be because I was leaving somewhere or the person I'm doing that with is leaving."

"No?" Chance asked.

"No. I'd want it to be because we both want it to happen, and we're ready for it. If that means we have to wait a while, I'd be okay with that."

"But if she's ready sooner, that would be okay with you, too?" Chance asked, smirking at her.

"Yes," Jo replied.

That smirk just did something to Jo. Chance didn't pull it out often, but when she did, it seemed to only be directed at Jo, and it made Jo picture Chance as the person that first time was with, which Jo shouldn't be doing.

"I just worry about Ruby's heart if this doesn't work," Chance admitted. "Long-distance is not impossible, but it's hard, and we're young. What if Jaden isn't the person for her? It's first love. How am I going to help her if that happens? If they break up? It's not like I have experience with this. *I've* never been in love."

"Does Ruby protect your heart in the way you protect hers?" Jo asked.

"Huh?"

"You're so worried for her."

"Oh. I guess she hasn't needed to. I've only dated a couple of guys, and that didn't last. It's not like I was how she was with Jaden over them."

"And if you were?"

"She'd be there for me," Chance replied. "She's my sister, you know? If I told her I needed her right now, she'd drop that phone and do whatever I needed her to do. And I'd do the same for her."

"I'm glad you have her."

"Who do *you* have?" Chance asked.

"You, I guess," Jo replied. "Not in the same way... Not like the sister thing. I just meant that—"

Chance laughed and said, "I get it." She paused. "I'm leaving in July, Jo."

"I know," Jo said, sounding disappointed now and unable to hide it.

"If I had known there would be this cool new person coming to town, I might not have signed up for the summer internship program."

Jo smiled at that and said, "No, you *should* go. It's important."

"Will you text me like crazy, like Ruby is doing with Jaden, probably right at this moment?" Chance asked.

Jo nodded but felt a little confused. Ruby was texting her girlfriend like crazy. Chance wasn't Jo's girlfriend, so it didn't make sense for them to text like crazy in the same way, but Chance had said it, and that had given Jo hope.

CHAPTER 12

"Hey," Ruby said, smiling wide.

"Hey. You look happy."

"Well, you're here," she replied, leaning in and kissing Jaden.

"And your parents are out of town," Jaden said.

"Yours think you're staying…"

"With a friend from school. I hate lying to them, but I wanted to spend the weekend with you, and I *am* eighteen years old. I want to be respectful, but if you and I had met, like, three months from now on campus, we would've been seeing each other every day."

"And *night?*" Ruby asked, hopeful.

"Well, you *do* have an off-campus apartment with your own bedroom, apparently," Jaden noted, wrapping her arms around Ruby's neck.

"I will, yes," Ruby replied. "And a roommate who will leave us alone every time you visit."

"We're not going to kick Chance out of her own apartment," Jaden argued.

"I didn't say that. She can be in her room; we've already talked about this. She even bought noise-canceling headphones."

Jaden laughed and asked, "What? Why would she–" Her eyes went wide. "How loud *are* you?"

Ruby laughed then and said, "Not loud, but I didn't exactly have a reason to be. How loud are you when you… you know?"

"When I touch myself?" Jaden asked.

"Don't say that. Now, I'm picturing it." Ruby looked skyward.

"You picture me doing that?"

"What do you think I'm thinking of when *I* do that?"

"Shut up," Jaden said, laughing. "And you know I've never done that with someone, so I have no idea what will happen. When I do… things to myself, I have to be quiet because my dads are in the next bedroom over."

"Do it when they're not home," Ruby suggested as she watched Chance's car pull up in the driveway.

"I do," Jaden said. "But I'm still quiet. I guess I've trained myself to be careful in case one of them gets home from work early."

"Too bad," Ruby said, kissing her quickly as Chance and Jo got out of the car.

"We don't have to watch you two make out all weekend, do we?" Chance asked.

"No, but I heard you already bought noise-canceling head-phones for the apartment," Jaden replied, pulling away from Ruby.

"Well, the way you two are all over each other, I wanted to be prepared," Chance reasoned, walking up the front steps to the house with her backpack slung over her shoulders. "Should I take the guest room with the–"

"Yeah. Jo can have the–"

"I know," Chance finished for her.

"Wait. Where am *I* sleeping?" Jaden asked Ruby.

"In my room," Ruby replied, wiggling her eyebrows. "That's all you brought?" she asked Chance.

"No, Jo is getting our stuff from the trunk."

"I'm chivalrous," Jo said, walking up with a roller bag and a big duffel bag. "But why she needs a backpack *and* a roller bag for two nights is beyond me."

"I brought two bathing suits," Chance argued.

"Yeah, like *that's* all that's in here," Jo teased.

"Hey, if you pick on me, I'm dunking you in the pool."

"There's a pool, too?" Jo asked. "There's a whole lake over there."

"The pool is heated; the lake isn't," Chance replied. "Come on. I'll show you to your room."

Chance and Jo walked into the house, leaving Ruby and Jaden on the steps.

"I'll carry your stuff upstairs," Ruby said.

"Okay. Should we get dressed for swimming? Will Jo and Chance want to go?"

"Let's give them some time to do whatever. You and I can go swimming if you want, though."

"Pool or lake?"

"Let's swim in the pool and then dry off on our blanket by the lake."

"*Our* spot?" Jaden asked.

Ruby smiled and nodded. Within twenty minutes, she was changed into her black-and-gold board shorts and a black sports bra. Then, she checked on Chance, who was taking Jo for a walk around the lake. The lake walk was a long one, and if they went the whole way around, it would take at least a few hours. Surprisingly, it was a warm but not a scalding hot day, so there was a good chance they'd make the full walk, which would give Ruby and Jaden all that time alone.

"I love that I have a pool," Ruby said softly to herself as Jaden took off her T-shirt and shorts, revealing a pink bikini beneath.

She climbed down the pool stairs and quickly moved into Ruby's arms.

"Chance and Jo, what's going on there?" Jaden asked.

"No clue," Ruby lied.

Jaden smiled at her and said, "Sure, you don't. As if Chance doesn't tell you everything."

"She tells me most things, but in her own time."

"What do you mean?"

"Just that Chance sometimes takes a while to come around to things. I'm a little more upfront about what I want or feel, and then I tell her right away. I guess I just say it as I think it sometimes."

"Yes, you do," Jaden replied, wrapping her arms around Ruby's neck as Ruby picked her up.

Jaden's legs wrapped around Ruby, and Ruby held on to

Jaden with her own arms at the small of Jaden's back.

"Is it annoying?" Ruby checked. "Chance tells me it's annoying sometimes."

"No, I like it. I pretty much always know what you're thinking."

"Want to know what I'm thinking about *now*?" Ruby asked, running a hand up and down Jaden's back.

"Probably not." Jaden laughed.

"I'm glad you're here. I missed you," Ruby told her honestly. "That's all."

"I missed you, too. I can't wait until summer starts."

"Do you think your dads will let you stay over then?"

"As in, sleep in your bed? No way. Not even if your parents are okay with it and sleeping down the hall – they're prudes."

"I'm not sure I've ever met two gay dads, honestly, but I guess I never thought they'd make a big deal about it. You're not a kid anymore, and it's not like we'd be having constant sex or anything – my parents would be right there."

"We *wouldn't* be?" Jaden teased. "Oh, that sucks."

Ruby smiled up at her and connected their lips for a kiss. They stayed like that for well over an hour, until Jaden said she wanted to get out of the water. Taking their towels and clothes, they kept walking to the lakeshore with the bag they'd packed until they reached the inlet.

Ruby placed the blanket on the pebbles again and waited until Jaden moved to lie down on top of it, kicking off her shoes and still only wearing her bikini top. She'd also thrown on a pair of jean shorts before, which Ruby now wanted to take off. When Ruby lay down on top of her, she hovered over her girlfriend, feeling like this might just be the best weekend of her life.

"Ruby?"

"Yeah?"

"I'm not ready for that tonight," Jaden said.

"For sex?" Ruby asked.

"Yeah."

"Okay," Ruby replied. "Can we just sleep next to each other? If not, there's another room you can—"

"No, I want to sleep with you. I'm just not ready–"

"You don't have to be. Jade, it's fine. Just because I've done that before doesn't mean you and I have to right now."

"I want other things. I've just never… I don't know that I really know what to do, and I'm worried I'll be bad at it."

"You won't be," Ruby said, pressing their foreheads together. "I'm… Jade, you know I've never felt this way before, right? I'm already talking as if you'll be visiting me at school, and I'll visit you, too, and that's months away from now. I can wait as long as we need to wait."

"Are you sure?"

"Of course, I'm sure. I'm a horny teenager; I can't control that, but I'd never pressure you to do something you're not ready for." Ruby thought back to something Jaden had just said. "Wait… You said you want other things. What did you mean by that?"

"I saw you," Jaden replied, looking down. "You didn't see me."

Ruby lifted herself up a bit and looked down at Jaden's bikini top.

"You mean…"

"If you want to," Jaden said.

Ruby nodded rapidly. Jaden laughed and sat up a little.

"Allow me," Ruby said, reaching for the strings at the back of Jaden's neck and pulling them apart. "Okay?"

"Yeah," Jaden said softly.

Ruby pulled the cups of the bikini down and licked her lips as she took in the sight of Jaden's perfectly round breasts with pink nipples that hardened when the breeze off the lake hit them.

"Wow! Is that stupid to say? That's dumb, probably. I just like… I like them," Ruby said. "A lot."

Jaden smiled and said, "You do?"

"I'm a breast girl."

"How do you know that?"

"Porn," Ruby stated.

Jaden burst out laughing and said, "See? I love that about

you. You just answered me honestly."

"I watch porn – lesbian porn – and boobs are… Well, it doesn't matter because those boobs are dead to me. I only want your boobs from now on."

Jaden laughed again as Ruby lowered her lips to Jaden's breast and kissed her hardened nipple.

"No one's ever…"

"Can I?" Ruby asked softly, brushing the nipple with her nose.

"Yes," Jaden said.

"And tonight, we'll just sleep, okay?" Ruby added.

"Okay." Jaden sighed as Ruby licked at her nipple.

CHAPTER 13

"How are you doing over there?" Chance asked.

"The humidity is getting the better of me, I think," Jo replied.

"It's not even that hot out today." Chance laughed.

"Says you."

"Well, we're too far along now to turn back; we might as well make the loop," Chance said.

"Why did I agree to walk around this lake?"

"Probably because you didn't want to have to watch Ruby and Jaden make out in the pool."

"Or, *more* than make out," Jo replied.

"Gross. You think they're having sex in the pool right now?" Chance asked, shaking her head.

Jo stopped walking and pointed. Chance followed the finger.

"No, because I think they're having sex over there."

Chance's eyes landed on Ruby and Jaden just as Ruby's lips were doing something to Jaden's breast.

"Okay. We're turning around," Chance stated.

It was a strange sensation that came over her. Really, it was a set of sensations. The first one was disgust because Ruby really was like a sister to her. The second was jealousy because Chance wanted that, too; someone to take those steps with. The third one was a weird one.

"You okay?" Jo asked as they turned on their heels and quietly turned around.

"Yeah. Why?"

"You just got really quiet there."

"Oh. Well, I've never seen my best friend... you know."

"We can just cut through here," Jo said. "Right? That way, we wouldn't have to go back around."

"Yeah, sure," Chance agreed, absentminded.

That third sensation was that pulse between her legs that

only came when she was turned on and thinking about touching herself when her parents weren't at home. She knew it wasn't because of Ruby or Jaden, specifically – it was more the act that she witnessed and picturing a faceless someone doing that to her because they couldn't keep their hands off each other.

"Can I ask you something?"

"Sure," Chance replied.

"You've never…" Jo hooked a thumb.

"No, I told you that."

"No, I mean *that*, specifically," Jo said. "No one's ever…"

"With my boobs?"

"Yeah," Jo said, laughing a little.

"I let a guy touch one over my bra once. He… Well, you can probably imagine what happened with him, and he kind of ran off after."

"What?" Jo laughed a little harder as they made their way through thick trees and underbrush.

"He couldn't stop it, and yeah…"

"He got hard and actually came in his pants?" Jo asked.

"We were fifteen. I think my boob was the first one he'd ever touched."

"Over the bra." Jo laughed further.

"Yes, and we were making out. He touched it, and I felt his… He pulled back and looked totally embarrassed. I told him it was okay; I didn't know what else to say. He ran off."

"Poor guy," Jo said.

They made their way through the trees and emerged on the single-lane paved road that Chance knew would lead to Ruby's house.

"You?" Chance asked her.

"Not even a hand on my bra," Jo replied. "No out lesbians where I'm from, and I never really had any close friends, either, so I couldn't even do the experiment-with-each-other thing if I'd wanted to."

"You didn't want to, though, did you?"

"No. This is the first time in my life I've even remotely felt like I fit somewhere and like working on this Pride festival might lead to more people my age coming out, talking to me, getting to know me, and me getting to know them."

"Is that what you want?" Chance asked, looking away from Jo now. "To… meet someone there?"

"Not like that," Jo said. "Not someone to date. Just people to talk to."

"You can't talk to me or to Ruby?"

"I can, but not about everything," Jo said.

"Oh," Chance replied, looking down at the perfectly kept lawn.

"No, Chance. That's not–" Jo stopped walking, so Chance stopped, too. "There's just stuff I haven't figured out yet, and I was hoping to meet more people like me. That's why I got involved."

"Ruby's like you," Chance replied.

"In one way, yes. But in many other ways, Ruby and I are totally different people. She's rich; I have holes in my shoes. She's outgoing and a leader; I read by myself for fun, and I am more of a follower. She's got this girl she's crazy about and went right for her; I have–"

"Hey," Ruby said from behind them.

Chance turned to see her walking up the hill with Jaden in tow and thankfully, fully clothed.

"Well, *that* was fast," Chance commented.

"*What* was fast?" Ruby asked.

"Faster than the guy who touched your bra?" Jo said just to Chance, who laughed.

"Nothing," Chance replied.

"We got hungry, so we were thinking about ordering pizza for lunch," Jaden added, looking pretty happy, so maybe fast was good in *this* situation.

Chance didn't know, but she followed Ruby and Jaden into the house, with Jo walking closely behind her. They played ping-pong and air hockey in Ruby's game room while they waited for their food, and after eating, they watched a movie together. Chance looked over and saw Jaden's head on Ruby's shoulder. Ruby turned to her then and smiled at her. She was just so happy. Chance smiled back at her and leaned into Jo's body a bit. She wasn't sure what made her do it, but she shifted just enough to rest her head on Jo's shoulder. Jo didn't move to wrap an arm around her, but Jo also didn't pull away, which was a good thing in Chance's mind.

The movie ended, and they went out to the pool to swim. Chance wasn't in the mood for water, so she lay on a chair and pulled out her phone to read a book. Jo dove off the board and made splashes like a kid at the community pool on the first day of summer, making Chance laugh, and Jaden and Ruby mildly annoyed because they just wanted to hang all over each other and talk softly as if no one else was in this backyard with them.

When it came time for dinner, they ate the leftover pizza and snacked on whatever they found in the house. They played a few board games after, watched some TV together, and then Ruby said she was tired, which was code for being ready to be alone in her bedroom with her girlfriend.

"Is my room next to their room?" Jo asked.

"No. You and I are down the hall, thankfully," Chance replied.

They cleaned up the kitchen a bit after Jaden and Ruby went to bed, giving them time to settle in and maybe stop making any sex sounds they might hear. Then, they headed upstairs and said their goodnights at their doors. Chance made a mistake, though. She'd always stayed at Ruby's house as a single guest, so the Jack and Jill bathroom that sat between two guest rooms hadn't been something she'd really noticed, but when she went to brush her teeth, the other door opened, and there stood Jo.

"Oh, shit. Sorry."

"I'm just brushing my teeth," Chance said through the toothpaste.

"I'll come back."

"It's fine," Chance said, spitting and rinsing. "I'm done anyway. I just forgot to lock that door."

"Yeah, I didn't know it was a shared bathroom," Jo replied.

"I kind of forgot." Chance shrugged. "Anyway... Good night, I guess."

"Yeah," Jo said.

Chance closed the door that led to her room and waited to hear it lock behind her. Then, she slipped into the cool sheets and stared up at the ceiling. A few minutes later, there was a knock at the door. Thinking it was Ruby who needed to tell her something, she told her to come in, but the bathroom door was the one that opened.

"Just wanted to say sorry again," Jo told her.

Chance laughed a little and said, "Jo, I wasn't naked or peeing; I was brushing my teeth. You can watch me brush my teeth."

"I know. It just could've been awkward. I should've–"

"*I* should have locked the door," Chance interrupted instead.

Jo walked into the room a little and said, "Think they're already…"

"Again? I mean, how many times can they go in a day?"

"Well, they're girls, so…"

"Seemed pretty fast in the woods, and I thought that was just a guy thing."

Jo moved into the room more and sat on the side of the bed.

"I have no experience myself, obviously, but let's just say… from what I've seen… places – it's a lot different when it's two women. Not sure what those two were doing out there. Maybe they didn't go any further than what we saw, or maybe they just got each other off quick, but when it's two girls, you can pretty much go all day and all night if you want. There are some things to… well, you can… get…"

"What?" Chance said, finding Jo's shyness to be so cute sometimes.

"Well, sore." Jo shrugged.

"Been there," Chance blurted out without thinking.

Jo's eyebrows lifted almost to that messy hairline.

"Not… I mean, when I'm by myself; when I was first… doing that."

"Oh, right." Jo shifted on the bed a little.

They'd changed into their pajamas hours ago, and Jo was wearing a pair of black sweatpants and a purple T-shirt that looked like it came in a pack of shirts because Jo had worn a blue and a green one identical to it before.

"You know, I couldn't stop," Chance shared.

"Oh," Jo said so softly, Chance almost didn't hear it. "Me neither. When I was…"

"First trying it out?"

"Yeah," Jo said, nodding a little. "It's…"

"Really good?"

Jo laughed and again said, "Yeah."

"But you wonder what it could be like with someone else doing that to you?"

"Yes," Jo said.

"Me too," Chance replied.

"What do you think it'll be like?" Jo asked her, shifting a little closer to the other side of the bed as if wanting to stay in here and keep talking to Chance, needing to get comfortable to do so.

"I have no idea." Chance chuckled. "I've heard that the first time hurts and is super quick, so not exactly great for the girl. Maybe girls should wait until boys are more like men and can–" Chance stopped when she took in Jo's face, which looked sad now. "That's with a guy, anyway."

"Yeah," Jo said, looking really uncomfortable now.

"What do you think it'll be like to be with a girl for the first time?" Chance asked.

Jo smiled and said, "I wish I knew. I guess I just want it to be special. That sounds dumb, but I think I'd want to touch her everywhere and, like, get to know her body. Is that weird?"

"Why would that be weird?" Chance asked.

"Just that it's sex, right? It's kind of got a purpose."

"Orgasms?"

Jo laughed and said, "Well, yeah."

"I don't just want that. Do you?" she asked.

Jo's head moved from side to side.

"Okay. Then, keep going," Chance encouraged.

76

She lifted the blanket next to her, inviting Jo to climb under it with her. Jo just stared at her at first but eventually moved to lie next to Chance, and they both stared up at the ceiling now, unable to look each other in the eye anymore as they talked about this.

"I want to find out what makes her feel good," Jo said softly.

"I think that's good," Chance replied.

"And I want to, you know, do things I've seen and heard about."

"Like?" Chance teased her.

"My mouth."

"Oh," Chance said, cheeks flushing at the thought.

"You don't want someone to do–"

"I do. I mean, I would," Chance interrupted quickly. "But... Do you worry you might not like it? Like the..."

"Taste?" Jo said as if not believing the word had just been uttered out loud.

"Yeah. I heard some guys at school talking about the girls they *say* they've done that with, and they talked about how they had to *deal* with that part or that it's–"

"I want it," Jo stated. "I want to taste her."

Chance's eyes went wide.

"Sorry. Too much?" Jo asked.

Chance turned her head then, seeing Jo stare at her.

"No," she said and swallowed. "Ruby and I haven't ever talked about this – not in this much detail, at least – and it's a little new to me."

"Me too," Jo echoed. "But I know what I want." Then, Jo stared straight into Chance's eyes and added, "And I know I want to make her feel so good, Chance."

"What about *you*?" Chance asked.

"Me?"

"Do you want her to touch you?"

"Yes," Jo replied.

"With her..." Chance licked her lips.

"With her everything."

CHAPTER 14

Jo hadn't slept well. She'd expected to be up most of the night because they'd all be hanging out like a normal sleepover. Jo hadn't been to many of those in her life, but the few she'd been invited to because all the girls in the class were invited, had been the all-night gossip-a-thons with talk about boys or clubs the girls were in. For Jo, they were awkward, at best, but she'd had much higher hopes for this weekend because it was with Chance, Jaden, and Ruby, and for the first time in her life, she thought she might just have real friends.

They hadn't stayed up all night, though. Today, they were going to work on festival stuff after breakfast before returning to the house, so they'd all gone to sleep around midnight. Well, she and Chance had stayed up until two in the morning, talking, and she was sure she heard Jaden giggle around that time, which meant that she and Ruby were still awake and likely doing something other than just talking, but even after Chance had fallen asleep, Jo hadn't left her room.

And Jo had planned to. When Chance's eyes had grown heavy, and she'd started to slow her words and then hadn't answered one of Jo's questions at all, Jo told herself to leave then. In fact, she'd told herself that over and over in her mind. Chance was out like an adorable little light. It was time to go. Jo had a room of her own. It was a nice room, too. It even had a TV in it if she wanted to watch something. She hadn't left, though. She'd just stared at Chance until she'd fallen asleep herself, but that had taken a while. And, as she woke, noticing the sun was already pretty high up for the eight in the morning they'd all planned to wake up at, she noticed something else, too.

Chance was half on top of her. Her head was resting on Jo's chest, rising and falling with Jo's breathing, which was coming in a little faster now. Jo's arm was also around her as if they'd rolled into each other a thousand times, and this was always how they ended up. Chance's hand was under Jo's shirt, resting on her hip, and it felt like this was how it was supposed to be; it felt like they should've been the couple giggling last night, too – kissing and touching until dawn because they couldn't keep their hands off of each other as they were alone, with a lock on the door, and without prying eyes or parental supervision.

Jo didn't know what to do, though, because this wasn't normal behavior for them, and while she wanted to stay this way forever, she didn't want things to be awkward when Chance woke up and realized she'd been snuggling Jo in her sleep. Slipping out from under Chance was an exercise in futility, but Jo moved slowly, and whenever Chance shifted a little, Jo stopped, waiting for her to fall back to sleep. Chance did every time, and then Jo was able to finally stand next to the bed, looking down at her. She grabbed her phone and left the room on her tiptoes until she closed the door quietly behind her.

"Mom," she said into the phone.

"Hey, honey," her mom greeted. "I'm off to work in a minute. Everything okay?"

"Yeah, I'm having a good time."

"That's good, Jo. I'm glad you've made such good friends here," her mom replied.

Jo had called her mom because she had no one else to talk to, and it had always just been the two of them against the world. After Jo's dad had died when she was three, her mother hadn't really even attempted to date. Jo knew it was because of her, and she hoped that once she was out of the house and on her own, her mom wouldn't worry so much about possibly bringing the wrong guy home or introducing someone to Jo and getting Jo to like them just for it to not work out in the long run.

"Mom, I have a problem, I think."

"Are you okay?" she asked, Mom-voice fully activated now.

"Yeah, I'm fine. I just–" Jo sighed as she sat on the sofa in the living room of Ruby's house. "I like someone."

"Chance?"

"How did you know?"

Her mom laughed and said, "Jo, you *only* talk about Chance. It's Chance this, and Chance that. *She's so smart, Mom. She's so funny, Mom.*"

"Okay. Okay." Jo laughed softly, looking around to make sure she was still alone. "I get it. I'm obvious."

"She doesn't like girls?" her mom asked.

"I don't know. She's of the opinion that sexuality is a whole thing. Her mom wrote a book about it or something. She's best friends with Ruby and doesn't have a problem with anyone being whoever they are, which is cool."

"But it doesn't mean she'd want to be your girlfriend?" her mom asked. "Honey, did something happen between you two? She's at that sleepover, right?"

"Yeah, she's here. But nothing really happened. We just fell asleep next to each other, and I..." Jo looked around again. "I woke up, and she was... She was kind of cuddling me."

"I see," her mom said. "Should I be worried about–"

"No, we didn't do anything, Mom. If we had, I'd be calling to tell you how happy I am and how I have a girlfriend, and–"

"Okay. Okay." The woman chuckled. "I'm still getting used to you not being home after school and going out with friends; you never used to do that back home. And I'm very happy that you are now, Jo, but tell me this... How did it feel when she *cuddled* you?"

Jo smiled at how hard that seemed to be for her mom to say.

"Perfect," she said.

"Oh, honey."

"I know." Jo clasped her hand over her eyes. "She's the only real friend I've ever had, Mom. I like Ruby – she's cool, too, but she has a new girlfriend, so I don't even really know her that well because she's busy with her and with the Pride festival."

"Okay. Well, Chance leaves for college soon, right?"

"Sooner than that. She has this summer program thing that's like an internship or something. She gets class credit for it, and it starts in July."

"That's not that far off, Jo."

"I know... And I know it's stupid to have feelings for my friend who's leaving soon, but I can't help it."

"Of course, you can't help it. You love who you love, Jo."

"I don't–"

"It sounds like you might be falling there, Josephine."

"Don't full-name me right now," Jo said.

Her mom laughed and said, "I didn't full-name you. I could toss your middle name into the mix if you–"

"Mom..."

"Jo, it sounds like this is serious with Chance; your feelings for her. You should tell her how you feel, honey."

"I can't do that."

"Why not?"

"Because it would hurt too much, and then I'd lose her."

"She's leaving soon anyway; you're going to lose her when she goes. At least, things won't be the same if you do tell her – she'll be in college and hours away."

"I know; don't remind me."

Jo heard footsteps and said, "I've got to go. Someone's up."

"Okay. Just... protect that good heart of yours, but don't be afraid to put yourself out there, either, Jo."

"Okay. Love you."

Jo hung up just as Ruby descended the stairs.

"Hey," Ruby greeted.

"Hi. I was just on with my mom." Jo held up her phone.

"Cool." Ruby nodded. "So, I might have possibly overheard just like a little bit of your conversation, but it wasn't on purpose. I was–" She pointed to the top of the staircase.

"So, you heard about..."

"Chance, yeah."

"Well, you knew already, didn't you?"

"Yeah. But it's worse than I thought, isn't it?"

81

"Worse?"

Ruby sat down next to her on the sofa and said, "I thought it was a crush."

Jo sighed and said, "I think we can safely say we've moved past crush at this point."

"You really like her." Ruby nodded again.

"Yeah," Jo replied.

"Listen, I know I kind of tried to warn you away a little at first, but I've seen you with her a bunch now, and maybe you should talk to her."

Jo was surprised by that and turned to Ruby then.

"I should?"

"It's complicated." Ruby shrugged. "Chance is a bit of an enigma at times, and she'll be moving away this summer. God, this will be the first time we've ever been apart for so long when she does her program. It's only a couple of months, and I'll be living with her after that, but it'll still be weird."

"Try finding her and only having a few months with her before she leaves," Jo remarked.

Ruby gave her a sideways smile and said, "Yeah, that sucks. I know; I just found Jaden, remember?"

"But at least you two are together already and have until you guys leave at the end of August."

"True, but that might just make it hurt worse. I know what it's like to really have a girlfriend for the first time now, and I'll be without her unless there's a school break or we can drive, like, six hours to see each other for a day and then drive six hours back. It won't be easy."

"But you're going to do it anyway."

"Yeah, I know my parents are calling it young love because they still see me as a kid most of the time, but Jaden just *gets* me. Chance has always understood most of me, but Jaden gets all of it. She likes that I blurt out what I'm thinking, that I want to be all over her whenever I can, and she wants that back. I don't care about people staring at us if we're holding hands on the street, and she doesn't, either. She likes me for me, and I like her for her."

"And you get to make out with her. Can't do that with Chance, huh?"

"Gross." Ruby shook her head rapidly. "I've never once been remotely attracted to Chance. Weird because she's gorgeous, smart, and all the things, but she's just the girl I grew up with and loved like a sister before I really understood what being with a girl meant. Jaden is… well, she's mine, and I'm hers, and that's all I really know right now."

"Chance isn't mine," Jo replied softly.

"Have you talked to her about how you're feeling at all?"

"No. She's my friend, and I can't lose that; I've never had friends. I'm the awkward person who likes girls and who doesn't really fit in with the girls *or* the boys at school, but I… I fit with her."

"I know. I can see it."

Jo smiled a little and asked, "You can?"

Ruby nodded and said, "Jaden was asleep when I had to go to the bathroom. I thought I'd go right back, but I overheard you talking and thought you might need a pep talk. I should get back now, but I *do* see it, Jo. I don't know what it means for Chance or if she's ready to admit it herself, but there's something there." Ruby stood then, adding, "And I'm a big fan of taking risks, so I say go for it, but I also know my best friend: it'll work out however it's supposed to, but you won't lose her."

Jo nodded and watched Ruby walk back up the stairs before she turned her head toward the back windows, where she could see trees swaying in the breeze and the lake beyond them.

"Hey," Chance greeted. "You didn't wake me up." She rubbed the sleep out of her eyes and walked over to the sofa.

"Oh, hey," Jo said, turning to watch her.

How much more was she expected to take? Chance's shirt was all bunched around her hips, and one pant leg was stuck in a sock. Her hair was in a messy bun, and her face showed she still needed sleep. She was absolutely perfect, and Jo wanted to push her down on the sofa and kiss her good morning.

"Why'd you leave this morning?" Chance asked as she sat down next to Jo.

So, she knew Jo had stayed in her room.

"Needed to call my mom to check in."

"Everything okay?" Chance checked, placing her head on Jo's shoulder.

"Yeah. We just agreed I'd call her a couple of times since there aren't parents here this weekend."

"Okay. Ruby and Jaden still out?"

"Ruby's up. She was down here for a minute. I think she went to wake Jaden up."

"Great. We have at least, like, twenty minutes. Want to make breakfast with me?"

"You cook?"

"No, but there's pancake mix, and I can add water."

Jo laughed and decided to go with Ruby's suggestion. It was a risk, but a small one that she could probably deny if she had to – she leaned over and rested her head on top of Chance's.

"If there's bacon, I can cook that. Eggs, too. I make them for my mom sometimes, but I can only make scrambled."

"I love scrambled eggs," Chance replied.

"Yeah?" Jo asked, breathing in the scent of Chance's shampoo, which smelled of mint and grapefruit.

"Do you add milk?"

"Yes."

"Perfect. I'm starving."

Jo lifted her head when Chance lifted her own. Chance patted Jo's knee and stood, stretching and revealing skin as she did. Jo stared but managed to look away before Chance noticed.

CHAPTER 15

"Morning, beautiful," Ruby greeted.

Jaden opened her eyes slowly and said, "You weren't here when I woke up, so I went back to sleep."

"I went to the bathroom," Ruby replied, sliding back into her full-sized bed.

"I like falling asleep next to you." Jaden snuggled against her side.

"Me too. I think I only want to fall asleep next to you now; no more sleeping alone. This will require you to come over here every night after your dads go to sleep and scale the wall. I'll leave the window unlocked for you."

Jaden laughed against her chest and said, "Well, since it's only for a few months because you'll be in an apartment and I'll be in a dorm then, I think I can manage that. Can you at least leave me a ladder or something?"

"Yeah, but I'll hide it in the trees."

Jaden laughed again and looked up at her.

"Morning," Jaden said, smiling.

Ruby leaned in and gave her a quick kiss.

"How did you sleep?"

"My nipples are sore," she said, flopping her head down on Ruby's chest.

Ruby laughed and said, "That's all you'd let me touch."

"Not true; you had your hands and mouth in lots of places last night. I think you managed to even make a mark on my stomach, and I do *not* have a one-piece bathing suit if we go swimming again today."

"I told you I was a boob girl." Ruby laughed.

"Well, you'll have to give them a break today."

Ruby moved until she had Jaden laughing underneath her and said, "I don't know if I can do that. I know what it's like to touch them now." She lifted Jaden's shirt up until she could see her breasts. "And they're just so perfect."

"They're boobs," Jaden said, glaring up at her playfully.

"Do you think *mine* are just boobs?"

"Let me see," Jaden replied as Ruby straddled her hips. She lifted Ruby's shirt enough to see them. "Definitely not *just* boobs."

"See?" Ruby said, laughing.

"How much time do we have before the others wake up?"

"They're awake. Jo was downstairs, and I saw Chance head that way when I came back in here."

"So, we can't get away with a few minutes alone?" she asked, running her hands up to cup Ruby's breasts. "I'd really like to just have, like, five more minutes where it's just you and me."

"Why did I invite them here? I'm so stupid. They could have come over during the day, but we could have had–"

Jaden's lips were around Ruby's nipple then. She was sitting up, sucking on it now, and Ruby lost all train of thought.

"Jesus!"

"There's a lock on the door," Jaden replied, kissing Ruby's chest until she found her other nipple and sucked.

"We should…"

"What?"

"Stop," Ruby finished.

"Why? I like doing this to you."

Ruby looked down when she noticed her hips were rocking against Jaden.

"Because of that."

Jaden stopped sucking and looked down. Then, she looked back up and smiled at Ruby.

"You did that last night, too."

"Yeah, and it's getting harder to stop."

"If you kept going, would you…"

"Yes," Ruby said.

Jaden leaned back in and sucked again.

"Babe, I'm serious," Ruby said, chuckling a little.

Jaden lay back down flat on the bed, which gave Ruby some relief, but not enough.

"Will you... do something for me?"

"Yeah," Ruby said, still trying to refocus.

"Come down here and kiss me while you do that thing with your hips."

"Jade, if—"

"I know. I want you to," she said.

"You want me to—"

"Is that okay?" Jaden asked.

"Would you do that for me? I mean, if I..."

"I don't know," Jaden said. "Maybe."

"Um... okay."

Ruby turned to look at the door she'd failed to lock when she came back into the room, walked over to it quickly, and locked it. She then checked with Jaden, who nodded, so she pulled off her T-shirt and watched as Jaden did the same. She climbed back on top of her, resting a thigh between Jaden's legs, and stared down at her as their breasts pressed together.

"Is this okay?" she asked Jaden as she slowly started to rock.

"Yes," Jaden replied, and Ruby watched her swallow.

"What do you want me to do?"

"Kiss me," Jaden said. "While you rock like that; it... feels good."

"Okay." Ruby leaned down and kissed her.

It was slow and steady at first, just like Ruby's now rolling hips. She could feel how hard her clit was as it rubbed against Jaden's taut thigh, and despite having a pair of shorts and her underwear on, Ruby knew she could come just from kissing Jaden and rubbing against her this way.

"If you want me to... you should... say something because..."

"I don't." Jaden's hand finally moved to Ruby's breast and

cupped it while her free one moved to Ruby's ass and held her there. "Don't stop."

"Will you?"

"I think so," Jaden told her.

"God," Ruby gasped out, pressing her own thigh harder into Jaden's center.

She wanted so badly to touch her, to slip her hand into Jaden's shorts and underwear and feel her, but she'd take this if this was what Jaden was ready for. Ruby moved her lips to Jaden's throat, her neck, and down to her breasts.

"Oh," Jaden said when she sucked on a nipple. "God, Ruby."

Ruby agreed with a moan against Jaden's breast. Then, she realized how wet she'd gotten. She had slept in a pair of boxers, and normally that would be all, but since Jaden was here, turning her on constantly, she'd added a pair of thin bikinis under them, and they appeared to both be soaked through now, which mean that she was now...

"Oh, my God. Is that..." Jaden pulled out of the kiss Ruby had just started.

"Yeah, sorry. I'm..."

"No, don't be sorry. That's... God, that's because of me?"

"Yes," Ruby said.

Jaden's eyes closed then, and Ruby lowered her face to Jaden's neck, rocking a little harder and faster now, needing to come because this was too much.

"Are you close?" she asked Jaden.

"Yes."

Ruby rocked faster and listened to Jaden's sounds, but then her ears filled with something else; the sound of rushing water, maybe. She was coming.

"Oh, fuck," she said, nearly falling on top of her girlfriend as she tried to keep herself balanced.

"Yes," Jaden encouraged.

Ruby *did* fall against her then. She kept her hips moving to ride out her orgasm as she buried her face in Jaden's neck.

"Oh, my God! Ruby, don't stop!"

"Shit," Ruby said, realizing at the same time that she'd come but that she still needed to keep the pace up for Jaden.

She placed her hand between Jaden's legs, cupping her and rocking harder.

"Yes!"

Jaden's hips rose and fell against Ruby's hand, and Ruby grunted because this was so fucking good, and they were still half-clothed and not really touching anything. Finally, Jaden's hips slowed, and Ruby stopped her own. She stayed just like this, with her face in Jaden's neck, for a long time, listening to Jaden's breathing and hoping that Jaden didn't regret what they'd just done.

"I can't believe we just did that," Jaden said after a few minutes of silence.

"Me neither. Is it okay?"

"Okay? It was so good, Ruby. So, so good."

"I didn't mean that part." Ruby laughed as she kissed Jaden's shoulder. "I'm glad about that, though. I meant the fact that we did that. Are you okay?"

"Yeah, I'm the one that started it," Jaden reasoned.

Ruby looked up then, able to face her knowing that they were okay, and smiled down at her.

"You…"

Jaden nodded and checked, "You?"

Ruby nodded and looked down.

"I think you're probably feeling the evidence of that on your leg."

"That's really because of me?"

"Yes," Ruby said, pressing a kiss to Jaden's forehead. "And I think we both need to take a shower before we go downstairs."

"Can you roll off me for a second?"

Ruby stared down at her in confusion but did as Jaden requested. Jaden moved on top of Ruby then, and her thigh was between Ruby's now. Ruby wondered if they were about to do this again with Jaden on top, but Jaden sat up a little and began moving back and forth on Ruby's thigh. Ruby knew what she was doing then.

"Is that because of me?" she asked, holding on to Jaden's hips.

"Yes," Jaden confirmed.

"My God," Ruby replied, closing her eyes. "A shower can wait. Keep doing that."

"We shouldn't," Jaden said. "I already want to take everything off you."

"Do it," Ruby encouraged.

"We can't," Jaden argued. "Chance and Jo…"

"Can wait," Ruby added. "I want you, Jade. I want all of you."

"I know. I want that, too. I'm not…" She stopped moving.

"Ready?" Ruby guessed.

Jaden nodded and said, "I'm sorry."

"Why are you sorry? This has already been the best morning of my entire life. Come here." She opened her arms, allowing Jaden to fall into them. "What we have is enough for me. It's more than enough. I don't want to rush this, either. I'm just eager. You're so beautiful, Jade."

"So are you," Jaden told her as she kissed Ruby's cheek. "But I don't want our first time… Wait… Does this count?"

"What?"

"Was *this* our first time? We both…"

"Oh, I don't know." Ruby thought for a second. "I don't know how that works exactly."

"Can our first time be when we're both fully naked, and our friends aren't downstairs?"

"Yeah," Ruby said. "We make our own rules." She winked at her.

"Hey," Chance said through the door, knocking after. "We made breakfast for your lazy asses. Get downstairs, and you better be fully clothed."

Ruby and Jaden both laughed.

CHAPTER 16

Jaden couldn't believe what they'd done that morning. She'd had her first-ever orgasm with another person, and Ruby had had one with her. Yes, Ruby had been with another girl before, but Jaden believed her when Ruby told her that it hadn't meant anything and that what she had with Jaden meant *everything*. Chance and Jo were in the lake, moving around each other and not actually swimming. Every so often, Jo would dunk Chance, or Chance would get onto Jo's back, and they'd stay like that for a while.

Ruby was sitting behind Jaden, kissing her neck every so often as she held her between her legs. Jaden watched her friends, the water, the trees, and the birds and couldn't imagine a more perfect day. Ruby's hand moved under her shirt and cupped her breast. Jaden smirked and laughed when Ruby squeezed it and played with the nipple through her bathing suit.

"You are relentless," Jaden told her, leaning her head back against Ruby's shoulder.

"Yes, I am. In all things, I think."

"Our friends are, like, fifty feet away."

"They can't tell what I'm doing." Ruby slipped her hand inside the bikini top. "And besides, they're clearly not paying attention to *us*."

"They really *are* cute together," Jaden noted.

"I hope Chance figures it out," Ruby replied. "I'd hate to see Jo get hurt."

"Jo's great. Head over heels for Chance, too." Jaden chuckled as Ruby's hand moved to her other breast, sucking on Jaden's earlobe. "Babe!"

"Come inside with me," Ruby requested.

"No way." Jaden laughed.

"We worked hard on festival stuff this morning, and you were giving me those eyes at lunch," Ruby told her.

"I was *not*," Jaden replied, laughing.

"They're having fun. We could…"

"Have fun, too? Are you suggesting we're not having fun right now?" Jaden asked playfully.

"I'm suggesting, we can have a different kind of fun." Ruby's hand moved to squeeze Jaden's breast again. "I liked what we did this morning. We could do that again."

Jaden wanted to do that again; she really did. But as much as she had loved what they'd done that morning and planned on doing that with Ruby again soon, she didn't want sex to become the main part of their relationship so soon. They still had so much to talk about and a lot of complications coming up in their lives.

"I want to," she replied. "But maybe tonight."

"Tonight?" Ruby checked.

"We have stuff we haven't been talking about, Ruby."

"We do?" Ruby asked.

Jaden turned in her arms, which meant Ruby's hand fell from her body.

"We have the end of the school year stuff, like our proms, and then the festival after that. Chance leaves in July, and I know you're going to miss her like crazy. We already live an hour apart, and I know it'll be summer, but my dads aren't going to let me sleep here or let you sleep there."

"So, we'll have some stolen moments," Ruby said. "We can always come out here, and my parents are gone a lot, so at least during the day–"

"And then we both move," Jaden interrupted her.

"Yeah, but we can deal with that later. Like, let's get through prom and graduation."

"*Proms.*"

"Huh?"

"I have one, and you have one."

"Oh, Yeah, I hadn't thought about that. Wait. Do you want

me to go to yours? I'm out at school, so I want you at mine, but if you–"

"I'm graduating; like I care what anyone there thinks," Jaden said, winking at her. "Yours is first."

"I was going to ask you."

"You haven't yet."

Ruby laughed and said, "Jaden, will you please go to my lame prom with me?"

"Yes." Jaden laughed, too. "And will you go to mine with me?"

"Yes," Ruby said.

"And we need to figure out the school thing…"

"I know," Ruby sighed, looking down at the blanket. "I know it's going to be hard, Jade, but I don't want to lose this."

"Neither do I," Jaden replied, placing her hand on Ruby's cheek. "I've mapped the drive. It's six hours and four minutes without stopping for gas, but there's a town about halfway between that has hotels. Maybe some weekends, we could just meet there. I'm going to get a job, so I can swing it."

"My parents are giving me an allowance because they don't want me to work freshman year. I'll make sure I always have enough money to see you wherever it is."

"Okay. How often?" Jaden asked.

"I don't know. I'd say every weekend, but–"

"That's not realistic," Jaden finished for her and sighed herself. "I know. We'll be in college – we'll want to be there for parties, football games, and studying."

"Yeah… But fall break is in mid-October, and we get there the last week of August for orientation. What if we did two weeks after that? I could come to you once, and two weeks later, you could come to me maybe, and then we'd be here for fall break."

"Or…" Jaden leaned in. "Is Chance coming back for fall break?"

"I don't know. Probably. Why?"

"Because fall break is only two days, and we could spend that long weekend at your apartment *without* your roommate."

Jaden leaned in the rest of the way and kissed her. "I'll be home for Thanksgiving, and I won't be that far away from my dads anyway, so I can visit them whenever."

"I really like that idea," Ruby told her.

"And home for Thanksgiving and Christmas, right?"

"Yeah," Ruby replied, reconnecting their lips. "What about after that? No school break until spring break…"

"Well, I'll want to be with you on Valentine's Day," Jaden said.

"So, every other week after New Year's Eve?" Ruby asked.

"And spring break together," Jaden added.

"And then the summer."

"Yeah."

"And do that all over again for three more years?" Ruby asked.

"That can be the plan for now, at least," Jaden replied, kissing her again. "And I like that you just said that."

"The three more years part?" Ruby asked, cupping Jaden's cheek.

Jaden nodded.

"Me too," Ruby said. "I just got really sad, though."

"I know," Jaden replied. "But we'll be okay. We'll figure it out."

"Yeah," Ruby said, but her tone wasn't convincing. "I want more time."

"Me too," Jaden replied, pressing their foreheads together. "Want to go for a walk around the lake, just the two of us?"

"No, I want to lie in bed and just hold you for hours."

"Oh, babe," Jaden said, kissing her. "Let's do both, okay? Walk first. Then, you can hold me during the movie I'm sure we'll watch tonight, and then we'll fall asleep next to each other again."

"Okay."

***

Their walk lasted for several hours, and they held hands throughout, stopping to kiss here and there until they made their way back to the house and found Jo and Chance sitting on the couch next to each other, watching something on TV. Ruby grabbed them all some snacks, and they stayed there for a long while until they were all tired and went upstairs.

Jo followed Chance down the hall, and Jaden noticed that Jo went into the guest room Chance was sleeping in. Jaden followed her girlfriend into Ruby's room. They each changed and settled in for the night. Ruby held her for a long time as they talked about their universities, what they were most and least excited about, the upcoming Pride festival and the impact Ruby hoped it would make on the community, and just about everything else.

Jaden was the one to initiate it. She climbed on top of Ruby, removing her own shirt in the process, and watched Ruby do the same. She spread Ruby's legs and moved her thigh between them. They were moving together moments later, and when Ruby came beneath her, Jaden watched her this time. She saw Ruby's face when she came undone, and Jaden wanted to be the only person to ever do this to her. Jaden slowed then, not yet coming herself but also not really needing to come, either; she'd just wanted to give this to Ruby. Then, as she stared down at her moments later, Jaden kissed her and knew she was in love.

CHAPTER 17

Chance wasn't sure what she was waiting for, but she was still waiting. She supposed she was just nervous to admit it out loud and take the step she'd been dying to take for over a month now. As she stacked white boxes filled with plastic forks, spoons, and knives in the corner of the storage area, she could only think of the fact that the prom, her senior prom, was in three days, and she still didn't have a date.

She'd already been asked by two guys at school. One of them was a former boyfriend, so that was a definite no. Their relationship, if it could even be called that, had ended for a reason. The other ask came from a junior in her history class. Chance hardly knew the guy outside of that room, so she'd told him no as politely as she could. Maybe she should have just said yes. Sure, it would have been awkward. The photos in front of the fireplace would have looked like two strangers attempting to get close enough to one another for the picture but being so nervous to actually touch, that when her dad said to smile, the worst prom picture in the world would've been taken.

Chance had said no, though, because this whole time, she'd been working up the courage to ask Jo – Jo, who was so much more to her than a friend now, and that scared Chance to death. All her talk of believing in love being love, finding her human in any shape, size, gender, and everything else, and Chance was having a difficult time reconciling with the fact that she was terrified of actually being with someone who wasn't the image she and her parents had had of the person she'd be with; the person who would take her to prom and kiss her at her doorstep after the dance.

Chance had been giving Jo the signals that she was interested in more. That second night at Ruby's, she'd asked Jo to stay in her room again, and she'd fallen asleep on Jo's chest. That had to mean something, right? Friends didn't do that. Ruby and Jaden had probably done that, but they were a couple. Jo hadn't said anything about it, though, and they'd woken up the following morning not acknowledging it and, instead, focusing on the Pride festival and hanging out with their friends.

At school, things were slowly coming to an end, and Chance knew that she'd miss the place. She knew she'd miss walking the halls with Jo, though, the most. Chance had come to expect Jo waiting for her after a couple of classes, and they'd walk to their lockers and catch up, despite having talked fifty-five minutes earlier on the way to class. They'd laugh. They'd find excuses to touch each other. Jo would hold on to her books for her while Chance opened her locker. Then, Chance would loop her arm through Jo's as they walked on.

"Hey, the carnival guy is here," Ruby told her.

"Okay."

"He's working out some details with my dad, but the rides and stuff are currently on the highway, making their way here."

"Yeah? That's awesome, Ruby. It's all coming together, huh?"

"Finally. I feel like I've been planning this for a year. The woman from the LGBTQ+ center suggested we do a parade next year maybe, *with* the festival, but that's so much work, and–ı"

"We won't be here," Chance finished.

"*I* will be," Jo added, walking into the room and placing a box of something on top of the ones Chance had just dropped off. "I think I said this before, but I'm game. I know I'm not you," Jo said, pointing to Ruby. "But I can help. Or, run it, plan it, whatever."

"You want to plan a Pride parade and a festival?" Ruby asked.

"Yeah. Why not? I don't want this to be one year and then never again," Jo replied.

"Neither do I," Ruby said. "Let's talk to her later. Maybe she can help."

"Yeah, cool," Jo replied. "I'll be right back; one more box."

Jo left them alone in the room, giving Chance the opportunity to talk to Ruby without Jaden or Jo for the first time in days.

"Hey," Chance whispered.

"What?" Ruby said, holding her clipboard and looking down at it.

"I have a problem."

"You have *many* problems," Ruby joked.

"Shut up." Chance laughed. "I'm serious."

"Jo?"

"What?" Chance's head went on a swivel, thinking Jo had somehow magically re-entered the room without her noticing, despite there being only one door.

"Jo is your problem," Ruby added. "Chance, just say it."

"Say what?"

"Oh, come on," Ruby said, laughing. "When we were twelve, and you liked that kid that always wore green, you couldn't talk to him. Remember? You asked *me* to tell him that you liked him and to see if he liked you."

"So?"

"So, do I need to tell Jo that you like her?"

"I–" Chance sighed. "How did you know?"

"Who *wouldn't* know?" Ruby countered.

"It's obvious?"

"Yes. Chance, is it the girl thing?"

"A little," Chance replied. "It's a lot easier to say I'd be great with anyone than it is to really understand that I'm, apparently, definitely not one-hundred-percent straight and act on it."

"I can see that," Ruby said. "But you've always been open to that idea."

"Idea, yes. Reality – I don't know."

"You like Jo. You *really* like her from what I can see," Ruby said.

"Yes."

"Do you want the things a couple does with each other with Jo? Can you see yourself making out with her and doing other things?"

"Yes," Chance replied.

She didn't specify that she'd touched herself just that morning thinking about Jo touching her.

"And?"

"And, what?"

"Good thoughts or bad thoughts?" Ruby asked.

"Good thoughts," Chance said, thinking back to them now.

"Okay. So, you like her as a person, and you're attracted to her."

"Yes."

"You should tell her."

"We're leaving, Ruby. We're moving, and I'm moving sooner than you," Chance reminded her.

"Then, enjoy the time you have left with her and use it to figure out what you both want," Ruby replied. "It's what Jade and I are trying to do. And yeah, it's sad sometimes to think that we're going to be apart for a while soon, but it's so good, Chance. It's just really, really good."

"You're assuming Jo wants me back," Chance argued.

Ruby just laughed – nearly cackled, really – and then left the room. Jo walked in with another box right after, smiling at Chance and dropping it to the floor.

"I overheard the guy saying the rides will be here soon, and they'll set them up and test them," Jo told her.

"Yeah," Chance replied, not really listening.

"Are you okay?" Jo asked her, running a hand through that sexy hair and making more of a mess of it than it had been.

"Yeah. Come here," Chance said, smiling at her and rolling her eyes. "You always mess it up somehow."

Chance moved her hand into Jo's hair, taking just a second to massage Jo's scalp and watching Jo's eyes close when she did.

"You like that?"

"Yes," Jo replied.

Chance massaged a little more, taking full advantage of the opportunity to touch her like this.

"Keep that up, and I'll fall asleep," Jo told her, leaning back against the boxes stacked high behind them.

Chance removed her hand.

"I didn't mean for you to stop," Jo added, opening her eyes and revealing them to Chance.

They were the perfect shade of brown with gold flecks, and Chance loved looking into them. She hardly ever could because then she'd be staring, and Jo would see her staring, and it would be a whole big thing.

"Will you go to prom with me?" Chance asked, unable to hold it in anymore.

"Prom?" Jo asked.

"Yeah."

"You mean, as friends?"

Chance put a tentative hand on Jo's right hip over the T-shirt and shorts.

"No," she said. "Not as friends."

Jo's eyes widened, and she said, "As a date?"

"Yes."

"I'd be your date?"

"Yes." Chance chuckled, placing her forehead on Jo's shoulder. "Is it dumb?"

"What? No," Jo replied. "Really? You really want us to go out?"

"Yes," Chance said as she felt Jo's arms slowly wrap around her waist.

"I'm not imagining this right now, am I?"

"No," Chance said, laughing again.

"Yeah, okay. I mean, yes."

"Yes?" Chance checked, pulling back to look into those eyes again. "We're going to prom together?"

"Yeah," Jo said, smiling at her. "I wanted to ask you. I've been working up the courage to do it ever since you told me you were going alone because you didn't want to go with those two guys who *did* ask you."

"I was working up the courage to ask you, hoping you'd ask me or–" Chance laughed at her own silliness. "I just wanted to go with you, and I didn't know who should do the asking."

"How long?" Jo asked.

"How long what?"

"Have you been…"

"Oh," Chance said. "A while now."

"Seriously?"

"Before Memorial Day weekend for sure, but even more for sure after that."

"Me too," Jo said. "I just didn't know if you'd actually want to."

"I do," Chance replied quickly. "I've never… Well, you know."

"Me neither, so… new for both of us, I guess."

"Well, hello," Jaden said, walking into the room. "Didn't mean to interrupt. The boss asked for everyone to come outside to get the plan for the rides and stuff."

"Do you call Ruby that in bed, too?" Chance teased.

"Not yet," Jaden teased back with a wink. "Also, not sure what's going on here, but feel free to carry on. I can tell her you need a minute." Jaden left them alone.

Chance leaned back into Jo, said nothing, and just enjoyed being this close to this amazing person with the promise of a date.

CHAPTER 18

"You look perfect," Jo's mom said, smiling proudly.

"You're not mad you had to buy me a second-hand tux and then spend all night fixing it so it actually fit me?"

"Not at all. I want you to be comfortable." Jo's mom took a picture with her phone.

"Mom!"

"What?"

"We're taking pictures at Ruby's house," Jo said.

"I know that. I just wanted one of you here first." She took another picture.

"Oh, my God!" Jo laughed.

"When you have kids one day, you'll understand wanting to always remember these moments." Her mom smiled. "You haven't had the easiest life, Jo, and I know having to help around the house and get jobs earlier than most kids made things worse for you."

"Also, the whole gay thing and being forced out of the closet by some stupid girl at school," Jo added.

"That too." Her mom straightened her black bow tie. "But you've been moping around for years, and this is the first time I think I've ever seen you excited about a school dance."

"It's also the first time I've had a date."

"Someone that you really like," her mom said.

"Yeah." Jo blushed. "She asked me. I still can't believe it."

"Why not? You're awesome, if I do say so myself."

"Mom, please do not embarrass me tonight. It's Chance's first date with a girl, and it's her senior prom."

Her mom laughed and said, "I won't embarrass you." She kissed Jo's forehead, adding, "I'm very proud of you."

"For what? *Chance* asked me."

"For always being yourself."

"It hasn't gotten me anything."

"It's gotten you a date with a girl you like who's never dated someone like you before, right?"

"I guess." Jo shrugged.

"And new friends who like you for you."

"Yeah."

"And, honey, I don't care if you wear a tuxedo or a dress to school dances or your wedding one day if you have one – I just want you to be who you are and to be happy."

Jo swallowed and nodded. She could *not* cry right now. She had to go meet Chance at Ruby's house.

***

Minutes later, they arrived in their old, beat-up car. Jaden's car was already there, and so was Chance's. There were also two other cars parked that Jo didn't recognize that, once inside, she learned belonged to Chance's and Jaden's parents.

"Hi," Jo said to Chance. "You look…" She took in Chance's short blue dress, which looked very soft, and shook her head. "Perfect."

"So do you," Chance replied, blushing back at Jo. "And I'll tell you more about *that* when our parents aren't watching us."

"Right." Jo laughed and handed Chance the corsage she'd gotten for her. "It matches your dress."

"Yeah? Thank you. Will you put it on me?" Chance said as Jo slipped it on her wrist.

"Hey, Jo," Ruby said. "Dapper in a tux."

"Who says *dapper*?" Jaden asked, slipping her arm through Ruby's.

Ruby was wearing a gray suit with a thin tie. Her hair had been slicked back, and Jo wished she'd thought to do something with her own hair. She hadn't known what to do and didn't have any products at home anyway, so she'd just left it as is. Her shoes were from the thrift shop, and her mom had polished them for her. Her bow tie, they'd bought at the *Super Target* one town over. It was a clip-on, and it kept going sideways. *Ruby* looked dapper; Jo looked like she'd tried her best.

Photos taken, they rushed out of the house and into the limo that Ruby's parents had rented for them. It was the first and probably the only time Jo would ever be in a limo, so she took it in as best she could. Ruby opened a bottle of sparkling cider. Jaden held out the plastic cups. Jo turned to Chance, who was staring at her with a smile.

"What?"

"You look hot. That's what I wanted to say in there," Chance replied.

"I do *not*. Ruby looks hot; I look like a mess," Jo argued. "Look at my hair."

"I love your hair," Chance replied, running her hand through it. "And I love doing this, too, so thank you for not putting a bunch of crap in it like Ruby did, so I can."

"Hey!" Ruby laughed as she passed them each a cup.

"You look hot," Chance whispered to Jo after they each took a sip. "And I'm so glad you're here with me."

"So, tonight… pictures, dinner, dancing, fun," Ruby said, holding her cup high. "One last hurrah before we ride off into the high school sunset."

"Well, *some* of us," Chance added, leaning into Jo.

"I still have another year of high school crap."

"Yeah, sorry about that," Ruby said.

The limo drove them to the hotel between their town and Monroe, which was where the class had chosen to have the prom. Jo held out her hand, taking Chance's and helping her out of the limo. She planned to let it go, but Chance entwined their fingers and held on. Yes, people stared. Practically everyone they walked by looked at them and probably wondered why Chance was here with Jo, and why they were holding hands, but it didn't seem to bother Chance at all.

They checked in and joined the line for pictures. Jo was nervous because the couples before them, including Ruby and Jaden, all held each other close, and she didn't know what

Chance would want them to do. She figured she'd take Chance's lead, and she was happy she did because Chance pulled Jo's arms around her waist, just like all the other couples did, and they stood there, taking a few pictures until their time was up, and they headed into the main ballroom.

Dinner was chicken and some vegetable Jo wasn't a fan of, but she couldn't really eat it anyway. She was trying to keep up with the conversations around her, and when they stood to walk around the room a bit, Chance kept introducing her to person after person. Jo was polite but wondered why Chance had made it her mission to introduce Jo around the party.

By the time the dancing had been in full swing for over an hour, and Ruby and Jaden had been on the floor pretty much the whole time, Jo had worked up enough courage to ask Chance to dance. Chance had pulled her over to a table, introducing Jo to the group who looked like they couldn't care less, and Jo was ready to either dance with her date, or sit the hell down and address the growing blisters on her feet.

"Are you okay?" Chance asked as they walked away.

"What is going on?" Jo asked back.

"What do you mean?"

"We haven't had a moment of just us all night. It's been table after table and then talking to people by the escalator. We haven't even danced yet, Chance."

"Oh," Chance uttered, stopping in the middle of the room between two tables.

"You haven't stopped telling people who I am or telling me who they are all night."

"They're all juniors, Jo."

"Yeah, it's the junior-senior prom."

"No, Jo… I mean, they're *all* juniors. Everyone I've introduced you to is a junior and will be a senior next year, when I'm away at school."

Jo understood then and said, "You're trying to help me make friends."

"You've spent all your time with me and Ruby. I just don't want to be the reason you don't make new friends."

Jo smiled at her and said, "I'll be okay, you know? I've been without friends before."

"I'm not saying you have to be friends with everyone or anyone you don't want. I just..."

Jo took a step closer to her, adding, "I appreciate you trying."

"I don't want you to be alone." Chance took both of Jo's hands.

"Will you just dance with me and worry about that later?" Jo asked.

"You want to dance?"

"Yes, to a slow song before my shoes tear my feet apart because they're half a size too small."

Chance looked down at her feet and up at Jo.

"Sit."

"What? Why?"

"Sit," Chance repeated.

Jo did. Chance sat in the empty chair next to her and kicked off the heels she'd worn, shoving them under the table. Then, she untied Jo's shoes for her.

"There. Off," Chance said.

"I can't just–"

"Yes, you can."

Jo kicked off her shoes and put them under the table next to Chance's. She stood, thankful she'd bought new socks, and followed Chance, who took her by the hand to the dance floor. Jo stood there, not knowing what to do for a moment, before she decided to take the lead this time. She wrapped her arms around Chance's waist and pulled her against herself. Chance's arms went around her neck, and she rested her chin on Jo's shoulder.

"Can I take my tie off next?" Jo asked.

Chance laughed, and Jo felt it everywhere.

CHAPTER 19

"Are you sure?" Ruby asked. "We don't have to."

"But I did a whole thing," Jaden replied, smiling as she ran her fingers over the back of Ruby's neck while they danced.

"You didn't *tell* me about this whole thing."

"I wasn't sure I'd be ready, and I didn't want you to get your hopes up if I wasn't."

"We can just—"

"Ruby, I got us a room. I had to do a whole thing because I'm only eighteen. I'm ready. My dads think I'm staying the night at your house because it would be too far for me to drive home. Call your parents and ask them if you can stay the night at Chance's."

"They're probably already asleep, but I'll text them that I'm staying there. Are you sure, Jade? We can—"

"I'm ready." Jaden pressed her forehead to Ruby's. "And I want to go now."

"Now? We're dancing."

"I know. I have the key already. We can get into the elevator and go."

"What about Chance and Jo?"

Ruby turned to see they were dancing close on the floor, not that far away from where they were dancing themselves.

"They can take the limo. We'll take a car home tomorrow morning."

"Tomorrow morning?" Ruby swallowed. "As in…"

"We're staying the whole night, babe. I'm not having sex for the first time and then picking my clothes up off the floor and going somewhere else."

"Sex?"

"What are you missing here?" Jaden laughed softly. "Are you still ready?"

"What? Yeah, totally. I'm just… I didn't think it would happen tonight. I thought maybe this summer before we leave. You're really sure this is what you want, and it's not just because we're all dressed up for prom?"

Jaden nodded and said, "I want to go upstairs and see all of you for the first time."

Ruby let Jaden take her by the hand through the dance floor, past the chaperones who weren't paying any attention, and to the elevator bank where they stood after she pressed the up button. Ruby pulled out her phone to text her parents that she was staying with Chance after the dance, and they got into the elevator. Alone, Jaden turned in Ruby's arms, letting Ruby hold her from behind. Ruby's heart was racing, and she knew Jaden could feel it.

"You're nervous," Jaden said as if reading her mind.

"Yes."

"Me too," Jaden said as the elevator dinged and the doors opened.

They walked out onto the floor with the ugly patterned carpet and way-too-dark wallpaper. Ruby took Jaden's hand, and they made their way down the hall until Jaden stopped them and turned toward a door. She pulled out a keycard, slipped it inside, and the door beeped. Ruby moved to open it for her, and Jaden smiled awkwardly, walking into the room. Ruby then let the door close on its own behind them, and it slammed way too loudly, interrupting the silence of the room.

They both just stood, Jaden slightly in front of Ruby, staring at the dark room and the bed they could barely make out. Ruby switched on the light by the door, giving them a better view, but neither of them moved.

"We can watch something," she suggested, wondering if Jaden had changed her mind, and wanting to make that okay for her.

"Like what?"

"Whatever's on," Ruby replied. "Late night TV."

"Can we sit?"

"Yeah."

Jaden walked to the bed and sat down on the end of it. Ruby sat down next to her.

"It's okay if you've changed your mind. We can hold each other or go back to the dance if you want."

"Ruby?"

"Yeah?" she asked nervously.

"I love you."

Ruby had been looking down at her hands clasped in her lap, but at those words, she looked over at Jaden, who was looking back at her with this intense nervousness in her eyes.

"I love you, too," Ruby said. "I've felt it from–"

"The beginning?"

"Yes," Ruby confirmed, letting out a nervous laugh. "You too?"

Jaden nodded and said, "And I want to do what two people do when they love each other tonight."

"Okay." Ruby nodded.

She didn't know how to begin. This was the most important moment of her entire life, and she didn't know how to go from hearing that Jaden loved her to them making love for the first time. Jaden stood then. Ruby thought she should stand, too, but Jaden motioned for her to stay where she was. Ruby watched as Jaden unzipped her red dress from the side and let it fall to the floor, leaving her there in a strapless bra and a pair of matching – yes, *matching* – red bikinis. It wasn't lingerie; it was just a matching bra and panty set Jaden had probably gotten from the department store, but it was the sexiest thing Ruby had ever seen.

"Oh, my God," she said softly.

"It's just like me in my bathing suit," Jaden replied.

"No, it's not." Ruby shook her head. "Way better."

Jaden went to wrap her arms around her body, but Ruby stood then and took Jaden's hands.

"Can *you* sit now?"

"Okay," Jaden said.

She sat on the end of the bed and watched as Ruby removed her suit jacket and tie. Then, Ruby unbuttoned her shirt and removed *it*, too. She stood there in her undershirt and pants, which she then unbuttoned after removing the belt. Jaden's eyes were darting all around Ruby's body. Ruby let the pants fall, kicked off her shoes, and stood there in her boy shorts and shirt.

Jaden stood then, pulling at Ruby's shirt until it was on the floor, and she was only in her sports bra and underwear now. Jaden cupped her breasts over the soft material, and Ruby closed her eyes.

"Off," Jaden said.

Ruby took the bra off, and Jaden stared down at her breasts.

"Off," she said again, eyes going lower.

"You're one-hundred-percent sure you–"

"Babe," Jaden interrupted, pressing her lips to Ruby's for just a second. "Off."

Ruby nodded.

"Oh, socks, too."

Jaden sat back down on the bed as Ruby divested herself of her remaining articles of clothing. Then, Jaden stared at her, and Ruby had this moment where she worried Jaden might not want this anymore. It was the first time Jaden would be with anyone like this, and Ruby was a girl. Would Jaden not really want to have sex now that she'd seen it all?

Jaden reached behind her back and unclasped her bra, letting it fall to the floor in front of the bed, and Ruby let out the breath she'd been holding. When Jaden moved back against the pillows, Ruby climbed on top of her.

"Can I take these off?" she asked softly, sliding a finger into the waistband of Jaden's panties.

Jaden nodded, nervously biting her lower lip. After Ruby removed them, she stared down at her beautiful girlfriend, wanting to do nothing more than make her feel good for every moment they had in this room.

"I love you," she said.

"I love you, too," Jaden replied.

Ruby moved until she was back on top of her, and Jaden opened her legs for her, letting Ruby settle between them.

"Oh," Jaden uttered.

"Oh, okay? Or, oh, we should stop?"

"Oh, okay," Jaden said. "I can just feel you."

"Yeah," Ruby said. "You told me you were ready, and I kind of... got ready... too."

"It's nice," Jaden replied, wrapping her arms around Ruby's neck.

"Are you not..."

"No, I am," Jaden said. "I am." She nodded rapidly.

"So, I should do..." Ruby pressed their foreheads together. "I don't know where to start."

"*You've* done this before." Jaden laughed.

"Not with you. Not like this," Ruby said seriously.

"Okay. Well, *I* don't know where to start."

"Can I touch you?"

"Yes," Jaden said, hovering her lips near Ruby's.

"Okay." Ruby took a deep breath and reached a hand down between them, cupping Jaden gently at first.

Jaden gasped against Ruby's lips.

"Should–"

"Ruby Simon, shut up and touch me already," Jaden said, cupping the back of Ruby's neck. "I love you. I want this, okay?"

"Yeah, sorry."

"Don't be sorry. Just– Oh."

Ruby slipped her fingers tentatively between Jaden's folds and watched as Jaden's mouth opened and her eyes closed.

"Oh, my God. You're so wet. I can... feel..."

Ruby closed her eyes as she kissed Jaden and began moving a finger up and down over Jaden's clit.

"That feels really good."

"Yes, it does," Ruby agreed.

"No, I mean, really good." Jaden's hips lifted and lowered, and then lifted and lowered again. "Like, I might... from just that."

"Okay," Ruby replied, watching Jaden as she moved beneath her.

She then stroked a little harder and a little faster and

couldn't believe the expressions on Jaden's face. She'd seen her come once before, but this was different. This was Ruby touching her in a place no one else had ever touched before. This was Ruby telling Jaden that she loved her by making her come. This was Ruby never wanting this with anyone else ever.

"Ruby! Yes!"

CHAPTER 20

Jaden woke with Ruby lying next to her. She smiled immediately and looked around. She was naked. Ruby was naked. Jaden was also a little sore, but not as much as she thought she'd be given everything they'd done the night before. Her legs were languid, and her arms felt like jelly at her sides as she looked at the girl she loved who had messy hair and had a scrunched-up nose.

"Shit," she whispered when her phone rang loudly on the table next to the bed.

"Huh?" Ruby said.

Jaden picked up the phone and rolled her eyes.

"Go back to sleep." She stood and made her way into the bathroom. "Hey, Dad."

"Hi, honey. Just calling to check in on you."

"I'm fine. You woke me up, though."

"Oh, sorry. Your dad and I wanted to make sure we'd see you later at the festival meeting."

"Ruby runs it, so… yeah, I'll be there. We're driving separately, so I can follow you and Dad home."

"Okay. Did you have fun last night?"

Jaden tried to figure out how to best answer that question. Had she had fun dancing with her girlfriend at the party? Yes. Had she had even more fun when Ruby had her mouth between her legs? Definitely. She couldn't tell her dad that, though.

"Yeah, we had fun. Lame school dance, but Ruby and I had a good time."

"Good. That's good. We'll see you later, okay?"

"Okay."

"And thank Ruby's parents for letting you stay over."

"I will," she said, wishing she hadn't lied to them but needing to have had the night with Ruby all the same.

She hung up and walked out of the bathroom, finding Ruby lying in bed with her eyes open now. They raked over Jaden, who realized only then that she was still naked.

"Good morning," Ruby said.

"My dad," she explained, holding up her phone.

"Are we busted?"

"I don't think so. They told me to tell your parents thanks, so there *is* a chance they're onto us. Will your dad be there to-day?"

"At the meeting? No. He and my mom have some church thing."

"Well, that's good." Jaden put her phone back on the table and slipped under the sheets again. "He asked me if I had fun last night."

"And what did you tell him?" Ruby asked, smirking.

"Shut up." Jaden laughed and rested her head against Ruby's bare chest. "I want more of this, not just one night."

"I know. Me too," Ruby replied, wrapping her arms protectively around Jaden. "You *were* talking about sex, right?"

Jaden laughed again and lightly smacked Ruby's stomach.

"I'm going to talk to my dads about letting me off the kid leash."

"You are?"

"I know it's their house, and it's your parents' house, too, so I want to be respectful, but in, like, three months, we'll be on our own. Had we gone to the same university, we'd be all over each other every night. I just want some freedom this summer, you know?"

"I know," Ruby said and kissed the top of Jaden's head. "We're supposed to meet Jo and Chance for breakfast in, like, two hours, and we don't have any other clothes here, so we have to go soon."

"Thank God I packed a bag for myself and left it in my trunk."

"I like that you planned this," Ruby smirked.

Jaden sat up a bit to look at her and said, "Yeah?"

"I was nervous that I'd somehow pressured you," Ruby

admitted. "We'd been going further and further. And you know I'm horny all the time and want to be all over you every second, but I didn't want you to think that—"

"Every step we've taken, I've asked you for it or told you I wanted it. Last night is included in that, and so is this morning." Jaden climbed on top of her.

"This morning?"

"I want one more time before we have to go."

"Just one?"

"How many times can we fit in, in like, thirty minutes?"

"At least two," Ruby replied.

Jaden leaned down and kissed her. Forty minutes later, wearing their dress and suit from the night before, they made their way to the shared-ride car they'd ordered, with their driver knowing exactly what they'd gotten up to last night. Ruby's house was empty, so they showered there together, which was something Jaden had seen in movies and on TV shows but never thought she'd be experiencing at eighteen. She smelled like Ruby's shampoo and body wash now, and that made it hard for her to stop smiling.

They arrived at the diner about five minutes late, with what her grandma would call shit-eating grins on their faces, and sat down across from Chance and Jo, who just stared at them for a minute without even saying hello.

"So?" Chance asked.

"Yeah," Ruby replied.

"And?"

"Her too." Ruby nodded toward Jaden.

"What are you two talking about?" Jo asked Chance.

"They love each other," Chance explained, moving into Jo's side and resting her head on Jo's shoulder. "Ruby said it, and Jaden said it back."

"That, and she got laid," Jaden added.

"Jade!"

"What? You *did*," Jaden teased her, placing a hand on Ruby's knee.

"I did. It's true," Ruby said, taking that hand and squeezing. "So, what did you two get up to last night after we left the dance?"

"We closed the place down," Chance replied. "I owed this one, like, fifty dances, so we just kept doing that until it was time to go. We took the limo back to your house, got my car, and I drove Jo home."

"And?" Ruby asked.

"And Jo kissed me on the cheek."

"Cheek? Really, dude?" Ruby said.

"Leave Jo alone," Jaden told her, laughing. "Cheek kisses are nice."

"They are, yes," Chance said, leaning up to kiss Jo on the cheek. "Agree?"

"Yeah, I agree," Jo replied, blushing.

"Did you guys order?" Ruby asked.

"Not yet. We were waiting on you two. Where exactly did you go?" Chance asked. "I know you weren't at your house; your parents were there last night."

"I got us a room at the hotel," Jaden revealed.

"How?" Jo asked.

"I know a guy who works there at the restaurant. He made the reservation in his name for me, I paid him, and he gave me the key."

"She's a secret agent," Ruby said.

"I wish I would've known; I could've covered for you. What if your dad called me or something?" Chance asked.

"I just texted them that I was at your place. Had they texted back, I would've told you, but they were already asleep. I got a text at, like, six this morning that they were going to church at seven and had some work to do there today, so they'd see me later. I love them, but they're always busy doing something, so I knew we'd get away with it."

"I can't wait for the days where we don't have to arrange things," Jaden said as their waiter approached. "Just you and me on fall break. Your apartment. Your bedroom," she whispered to Ruby when the waiter asked Chance what she wanted to drink.

Then, Jaden watched Ruby swallow.

They ate breakfast together, talking about the dance and how people had made comments and asked questions but hadn't been rude to any of them for the gender of their dates. That, Jaden knew, made Ruby happy because she was big on leaving the place better than how she found it, and Jaden loved that about her.

After breakfast, it was time to go to the festival grounds, where things were being set up and tested. Ruby had her clipboard in hand and was assigning jobs to everyone during and after the meeting, while Jaden tried to avoid her dads for as long as she could because she knew they'd have a million questions about the dance, but they eventually cornered her by the ringtoss game she was helping to set up.

"Hey, honey."

"Hi, Dad," she said.

"So, how was it?" her other dad asked.

Jaden knew he wasn't talking about sex, so she had to put that thought and how she'd answer the question out of her mind.

"Good. We had fun."

"Did you take lots of pictures?"

Jaden cleared her throat then. She had taken several pictures at the dance, but she'd also taken one of her with Ruby after their last round in the hotel bed. They were naked but had the white sheet up to their necks. They'd turned to each other at the same time, with Jaden holding the phone over her head, and they'd kissed.

"I did. But I still need to sort through them, so I can show you some later," she replied.

"Great. We're looking forward to it. We have a meeting with the hotline group, so we'll see you when it's time to go."

"Okay," she said.

They walked off just as Ruby approached.

"Penny for your thoughts."

"It's five dollars for twenty rings, actually," Jaden joked, walking over to the rope that separated Ruby from her.

"I have a feeling, if I get you a ring one day, it'll be more than five dollars."

"Oh, that's a good one," Jaden replied, leaning over and giving her a kiss. "And my thoughts are all good right now. Yours?"

"All good," Ruby said. "I can't believe this is about to happen." She looked around the festival grounds.

The rides were all up and being tested. The games were nearly set. The food, music, and booths were all just about ready, too. Jaden's girlfriend had breathed this thing into life and was about to make a major impact on the lives of people who probably didn't know where they fit or knew who they were but hadn't said anything yet out of fear or confusion. Ruby was amazing.

"Hey."

"Yeah?" Ruby said.

"I love you."

Ruby smiled at her and said, "I love you, too."

CHAPTER 21

Chance found Jo over by the balloon pop booth, talking to one of the guys who worked for the carnival company. She approached Jo from behind and tickled her sides.

"Hey!" Jo turned around with an angry face until she realized it was Chance, and her anger turned to happiness.

"Sorry, I was trying to be funny."

"I didn't know it was you. I'm still getting used to someone touching me," Jo said.

"Oh, yeah?" Chance asked.

"I've got to get back to work," the guy behind Jo said.

"So, want to test some more games with me?" Chance asked, hands at Jo's hips. "Jaden has the ring toss ready, and if you hit the middle bottle, you get twenty bucks."

"It would cost me a thousand to get those twenty bucks," Jo replied.

"We get to play for free – well, today anyway, since it's not really open, and you won't actually win the money, but it'll be fun."

"Okay. Sure. Ruby hasn't given me a new task yet."

"Then, let's go before she finds us."

Prom night had ended after they'd danced more times than Chance could count. They'd taken a break, and a few people had approached them to say hello. A couple of them had been juniors and had spent time with Jo, which made Chance happy. She was trying not to worry about Jo being here on her own once she left in July. She knew Ruby and Jaden would still be here for another couple of months, but they were together and wanted to spend as much time alone as possible before they had to go their separate ways.

"So, can we talk?" Jo asked.

Chance looked down at her feet as they walked through the trampled-on grass, worried at Jo's words.

"Um… Yeah. Sure."

"It's just that we're hanging out, and we had a date… I don't know what happens next, so I wanted to ask you, maybe, what you wanted."

"What I wanted?" Chance asked, stalling.

"With me? With *us*?"

"Oh, right," Chance said.

"It's okay if it's nothing. If you want to go back to being friends–"

"What? No, I don't want that," Chance replied as she stopped walking.

"You don't?" Jo stopped next to her.

"No. We've been on one really good date, and I want to go out again."

Jo smiled and said, "Okay. When?"

"I don't know. Graduation and the festival mean I'll be pretty busy for the next couple of weeks."

"And then you leave," Jo added, looking off at the rides and games in the distance.

"We can figure it out," Chance replied, taking Jo's hand. "I *want* to figure it out."

"Okay. School night dates?"

"Dates *plural*, huh?" she teased, moving into Jo.

"Yeah. Like, Monday night, we could go to dinner. Maybe Tuesday, we could see a movie. Wednesday, we could go to the lake. Thursday, my mom works late, so you can come over, and we can just watch TV or something. Not romantic, but we'd be alone, and–"

"You've got it all planned out, huh?" Chance smirked.

"What about Friday night? Graduation isn't until Sunday."

"I'm having dinner with my parents Friday night, but maybe after, you could come over."

"Will they be there?"

"Yes," Chance said, laughing at her.

"Maybe we could go somewhere, then. *Carver's*?"

"Okay, ice cream on Friday night. My open house is on Saturday, so I'll see you then, and after I help my parents clean up the house, we could do something."

"Yeah," Jo said, smiling, but it didn't meet her eyes. "Festival the next weekend."

"Jo, I want every free moment I have with you, okay?"

"What happens after, though?"

"After I leave?" Chance checked, knowing the answer already.

"Yeah. I'm going to get a summer job to help my mom out. I had one before, but I've been putting it off because I just got here and needed to catch up. And then, I wanted to spend as much time with you as possible, but we could really use the money. I might even get two jobs if I can, so that doesn't leave me much time to visit."

"I'll come back once before school starts. My parents and I are trying to work out the weekend. I still have to do the back-to-school shopping thing, and we need to get things for the apartment."

"So, I could see you that weekend?"

"Yeah, I'll just do a bunch of shopping online before that weekend so that we don't have much to get in person, and that'll give us more time."

"And more time as what, exactly?" Jo asked.

Chance wrapped her arms around Jo's neck and pulled Jo in for a hug.

"I don't know that yet. But I do know that I don't want to be without you." Chance pressed hesitant lips to Jo's neck, tasting a bit of sweat from the heat and their work so far that day.

"I don't want to just be your friend, Chance. If you're not ready to be something more, with an actual label, that's okay, but I *want* to be more."

"More... like, girlfriends?" Chance asked her, still holding on to Jo, who was hugging her back tightly now.

"Yes."

"Well, can we start with dating and see how that goes?"

"Sure."

"So, we're officially dating, not just friends anymore, and that means I get to hold your hand."

Jo chuckled against Chance's body and said, "Yes, you can hold my hand, but you held my hand when we were friends, too."

"Yeah, but now it means more," Chance argued.

"I think it meant a lot when we were just friends, but sure," Jo replied.

Chance pulled back and looked into Jo's eyes. She wanted to kiss her, and not just on the cheek. She'd been thinking about it more and more recently, even before their prom first date. She loved Jo's eyes, her lips, her neck, and how it felt to have her face buried against it – safe and cared for. She also loved touching Jo on her hips. For whatever reason, that was her favorite spot to have her hands on Jo's body. She moved a hand to Jo's right hip now, sliding it under her T-shirt and resting it against the bone she found there. Then, she let her thumb graze the skin and watched as Jo's eyes closed. Chance rubbed the back of Jo's neck with her left hand, knowing they were in public and couldn't do anything else; she didn't want their first kiss to be in front of strangers from a carnival company.

"I like when you do that," Jo said.

"Me too," Chance replied.

"I've been trying *not* to touch you."

"What? Why?" Chance asked.

"Because we were friends, and I was crazy about you and didn't want to give that away."

Chance smiled up at her adoringly and said, "Now that we're dating, where do you want to touch me?"

"Oh, I *can't* answer that question here."

Chance laughed and said, "PG locations only, then."

"Here," Jo said, cupping Chance's cheek. "And here." Her other hand went to Chance's neck, and she held her in place just like that as she stared into Chance's eyes. "And I want to touch you here, obviously." Jo moved the thumb from Chance's cheek and let it graze over her lips.

Chance gasped and nearly took that thumb into her mouth

accidentally before she closed her mouth.

"I'd like that," she said softly.

"And here," Jo added, lowering a hand to Chance's hip. "I have this thing where I picture myself putting my fingers through your belt loops and tugging you toward me."

"You do?" Chance asked, thinking that was really cute.

"Yeah. Stupid?"

"No. You can... whenever."

"Okay. Well, you're already standing really close, so maybe later."

"Okay," Chance said. "Where else?"

"Um... here." Jo's hands moved to her hips and a little under Chance's shirt to touch skin.

"Yeah, I like that spot on you, too."

"When we were swimming in the lake, I really wanted to pick you up."

"You did," Chance reminded, recalling the hours they'd spent in the water.

"I gave you piggyback rides – I wanted to pick you up how Ruby picked Jaden up."

"Jaden was in front of her," Chance recalled. "And they were..."

"Kissing and holding each other," Jo finished for her.

"I want that, too," Chance replied. "I might just need to take some of those things slow."

"Okay. I'm okay with that. I've never done any of this stuff, either."

"We'll have our firsts together, then," Chance said. "Some of them." Her eyes went wide. "I don't mean all of them. Well, I don't know. Maybe we... Sorry. I wasn't planning to meet someone right before I moved away."

"It's okay. I wasn't planning on even making friends, and here I am, dating the only real friend I've ever had," Jo said. "We'll take this slow."

"But I'm leaving."

"And I don't want to rush something just because of that, remember?"

"Yeah, me neither. If we're both ready, though, maybe," Chance said, pressing her face into Jo's chest. "Don't stop yourself from touching me, though, okay?"

"You're okay with PDA?"

"Yes," Chance replied. "We're standing in the middle of a field with, like, a hundred people walking around – pretty sure I'm good with you touching me in public like this."

Jo's arms wrapped protectively around her, and Chance wanted to melt into them.

"You're beautiful, Chance. I've wanted to say that so many times – just so beautiful – and I can't believe we're doing this."

"When I called you hot on prom night, did you like that?" Chance asked.

"Who *wouldn't* like that?" Jo asked, laughing.

Chance pulled back to look at her and said, "Well, you called me *beautiful*, but I don't think you'd necessarily like me calling you that word, would you? *Handsome* applies, but it doesn't really seem to suit you, either. I mean, I think you're beautiful, gorgeous, handsome, sexy, hot, and just about everything else, too. Adorable and cute also work for me, but I want to use the words you'd want me to use when I describe you. So, hot? Sexy? Gorgeous?" Chance ran her hands up over Jo's chest, not stopping on her breasts, but feeling them through the shirt before she breezed past them and wrapped her arms back around Jo's neck. "Beautiful? Handsome?"

Jo looked at Chance as if no one had ever asked her this question, and she had no idea how to answer it.

"However you want to describe me is fine. I don't know that I think any of those words really apply to me."

"Then, I'll keep saying them until you do," Chance replied.

Jo kissed her forehead and hovered there for a moment.

"Come on, sexy. Let's go find Ruby and her clipboard," Chance said, laughing.

CHAPTER 22

The festival was finally here, and Jo had been hard at work for hours now. Her feet were killing her. She was sweating. She was tired, and she hadn't seen Chance in hours. Jo had worked a two-hour shift at one of the games, and another few hours in the main food tent, bouncing from the funnel cakes to the corn dogs and back. Then, she'd gone to the raffle and craft tent where they were featuring work of queer artists.

Jo talked to one of the artists who was there to sell their work, and she felt drawn to them in a way – not in the way Jo felt drawn to Chance, but in the way that she wanted to learn more. So, during her shift, Jo had asked them some questions.

"So, you're non-binary *and* a lesbian?" Jo asked.

"Yes," they said.

"How can you be both? I'm just starting to learn this stuff, so I don't know. Sorry, that's personal and probably sounds like–"

"It's different for everyone. I don't feel like I'm a man or a woman – I don't fit those stereotypes, I guess. And I'm attracted to women; I've never been with a man."

"Right. So, you use *they* and *them*?"

"Yes," they replied, smiling at Jo. "Can I ask why you're asking?"

"Oh, just curious. I don't know any non-binary people. I'm not really sure how it works."

"Do you *want* to know?" they asked, smiling softly at Jo.

Jo sat down in the chair next to them and said, "Is it obvious?"

"Yes, but not to everyone, most likely. Isn't that the point of this festival? Open up conversations, learn about each other, and support our causes?"

"Yeah, I guess. I'm here because of that, I think. I mainly

signed up to help at first because I know I'm gay – only girls for me."

They laughed and said, "I get that. What about the other thing?"

"The gender thing?" Jo asked.

"If you don't want to talk here, I'm happy to give you my card. You can email me or call me, and we can talk in private."

"I don't know if I'm ready to talk or, I guess, *be* anything. I sometimes still think of myself as a girl. When people say *she* to me, it's fine. Not a big deal, but it doesn't feel…"

"Right?"

"Yeah," Jo said, grateful.

"Whoever you are is up to you," they replied. "And if you ever want to talk, you can always reach me here." They handed Jo a business card.

"How does it impact your… relationships?"

"Being non-binary or being a lesbian?"

Jo tucked the card into the back pocket of her jean shorts before clarifying, "The non-binary thing."

"I'm pretty open about it – I have to be if I expect people to know my pronouns. If I'm interested in a woman and she's not accepting, it pretty much ends there. But I'm lucky – I met an amazing woman not long after I came out as non-binary, and we've been married for two years now," they said. "I think you just find the person who accepts you for who you are."

"Hey," Ruby said, walking up to the table. "I'm here to relieve you. Break time."

"Oh, okay," Jo replied.

Then, Jo looked at the artist and nodded with a smile. The artist nodded back, and Jo stood up and walked around the table.

"And Chance is on break, too, so feel free to track her down inside the community center and take your breaks to-gether," Ruby added.

"Thanks," Jo replied, laughing. "I appreciate it."

Walking into the community center, Jo found Chance talk-ing to an older woman in the hallway. Jo approached from be-hind her and tapped Chance on the shoulder.

"Hey, you," Chance said, smiling.

"Hi. We're on break now; Ruby asked me to tell you."

"Oh, cool," Chance replied.

She then said goodbye to the woman she was talking to before and took Jo's hand.

"Want to hop on some rides with me?" Chance suggested as they headed outside. "We can skip the line."

"Yeah, let's do it," Jo agreed.

They made their way back outside, and Jo listened as Chance talked about her day so far. She'd helped set up things for the hotline and then spoke to one of the women from the LGBTQ+ center, asking her questions about how she should identify now that she was dating Jo.

"What did she say?" Jo asked curiously.

"She told me that my identity is my own – which I know, obviously, but I don't know if I'm bisexual or something else."

"You don't have to know yet – or ever, really."

"Yeah," Chance said and then added, "Does it bother you?"

"Does *what* bother me?"

"That I'm not gay?"

"What? No," Jo said, stopping them near the elephant ear stand.

"Are you sure? I don't know that I'm strictly bisexual. Pansexual is something I've entertained. I think I need to do more research. I'll talk to my mom, too."

"You're going to talk to your mom about maybe being pansexual?" Jo asked.

"I talk to my mom about most stuff," Chance replied. "She's studied and done research on human sexuality."

"Do you think she's going to be bothered by it?"

"She didn't care that I took *you* to prom."

"Probably because I looked like a guy in the pictures, so she could always tell people in, like, ten years that your prom date was a boy."

"Jo," Chance said, shaking her head. "My mom's not like that. She knows we're dating, and she hasn't pressured me to tell her that I'm anything. She's open, too."

"Open?"

"She met and fell in love with my dad, but she dated women, too, before they met."

"What?" Jo asked.

Chance laughed and said, "My mom is bisexual, Jo; always has been. Always will be even though she married my dad."

"I didn't know."

"Why would you?" Chance replied. "It's one of the reasons she studied what she did. Anyway... I don't know yet how I identify, and I'm okay with that. I was just hoping you would be, too."

"Yeah, I'm fine with it. I just like *you*," Jo said.

"Good." Chance smiled. "Ferris wheel?"

"Okay," Jo replied, letting Chance walk them, holding hands, through the crowd that had grown substantially since the sun had set and the lights of the festival rides and booths had all turned on.

Chance waved at the guy who was running the wheel, and he nodded back in acknowledgement and waved them through. Within a minute, they were in a car, and Jo's arm went around the back of it as Chance rested her head on Jo's shoulder.

"I've never ridden one of these things with someone I was dating," Chance shared as the car moved once to allow the next car to be filled.

"Me neither, obviously."

"I kind of have this cliché vision of what happens when we get to the top."

"Vision?" Jo asked, trying to keep up as the car moved again.

"Yes," Chace stated. "I was thinking that maybe you could kiss me."

Jo swallowed hard and said, "You want me to kiss you at the top?"

"And not on the cheek," Chance added, placing her hand on Jo's stomach.

"Forehead?" Jo joked.

"Nope."

"Nose?"

"Nope."

"Hand?"

Chance laughed and said, "Nope."

When the car moved again, Jo placed a hand on Chance's shoulder and rubbed it a bit. Then, Jo waited until the car moved again. One more time, and they'd be at the top of the wheel, where Chance wanted Jo to kiss her. Jo's mouth was dry. Jo couldn't remember the last time *they* had a drink of something, but even if they'd just downed a whole bottle of water, their mouth would still be dry.

"Um… Chance?"

"Yeah?"

Jo bit their bottom lip as the car moved again.

"I've never kissed anyone before."

Chance lifted her head and looked at Jo.

"No one?"

"No."

"I'm going to be your first kiss?" she asked, smiling.

"If you still want to—"

Chance's lips were on Jo's then. Jo hadn't expected it, so their mouth had been half-open, and Chance's lips had landed more next to their mouth than actually on it. An instant later, Chance's hand was on the back of Jo's neck, pulling Jo into her. Jo finally moved their lips, unsure of what to do, so they just went with whatever Chance was doing.

It didn't last long. Chance pulled back, and Jo worried they'd done something wrong until they saw Chance's smile. Jo leaned back in this time, taking Chance's bottom lip between their own and letting it go. Chance reconnected their lips as the car began to move. Jo thought they'd separate when they got to the bottom, but Chance kept kissing Jo, so Jo kissed her back. Their hand moved to Chance's thigh, resting on the skin below the hem of her shorts. Chance's hands were now in Jo's hair, messing it up even more than it usually was, and around and around they went.

Jo took a chance and moved their lips to Chance's jaw on the third time around. When Chance didn't object, Jo moved them a little farther down and over to her neck, which they kissed as they went around for the fourth time. They heard Chance gasp a bit as they lowered their lips to Chance's shoulder, and Jo's teeth more bumped it than anything, but when Chance gasped again, Jo decided to nibble a little on the salty skin they found there.

"Jo," Chance said breathlessly.

"Sorry," Jo replied, stopping immediately.

"What? No, keep going," Chance said, pressing Jo's head back against her neck. "I was just saying your name because…" Chance didn't finish as Jo sucked on the skin of her neck. "Okay… I can't go home with a hickey." She laughed a little.

Jo moved their lips back to Chance's, kissing her as their car stopped at the top, letting the people off the Ferris wheel below them. Chance kissed Jo back harder as if she realized they'd have to stop soon.

"What time do you have to be home tonight?" she asked, moving her own lips to Jo's neck.

"Midnight." Jo leaned their head back as the car moved.

Then, Jo closed their eyes, not believing this was happening, as Chance's hand moved up under their shirt and rested on their abdomen.

"Make out in my car before you have to go home?" Chance asked.

"Yes," Jo replied. "Definitely."

CHAPTER 23

"We can't," Ruby said.

"Yes, we can," Jaden replied, shoving Ruby into the storage closet. "We're on a break."

"I don't get a break; I'm in charge," Ruby argued, laughing as Jaden closed the door behind them and locked it.

"Babe, come on," Jaden said, flicking on the light switch. "We have at least ten minutes before someone notices we're gone. At least, make out with me."

Ruby opened her arms for Jaden to walk into.

"Lame to say that I've missed you?" Ruby asked.

"No," Jaden said, wrapping her arms around Ruby's neck. "I've missed you, too."

She used her knee to push Ruby's legs apart and pressed a thigh between them.

"Jade!"

"What? I want you. Are you really surprised?"

"We're in a storage room," Ruby remarked.

"So?" Jaden pressed her thigh to Ruby's center.

"Not exactly romantic."

"Ruby, I don't need romance right now. I just... I want you to touch me." Jaden rocked into her. "I don't know when we'll get another moment like this; you're working all weekend. And so am I, because I love you and I want to help here. But then, it's graduation, and I'm an hour away, and my dads won't let me just—"

"Okay. Okay," Ruby said. "You're right." She leaned in and pressed her lips to Jaden's, turning them around until Jaden was pressed against something she couldn't see.

Ruby's hands were on her shorts now, undoing them and slipping inside. Jaden's head went back as Ruby kissed her neck.

"I love you," Ruby told her.

"Then, touch me already," Jaden said, smiling with her eyes still closed.

Ruby laughed against Jaden's skin and moved her hand into her girlfriend's underwear.

"How long have you been like this?" she asked, stroking Jaden now.

"Since I watched you directing everyone like you're fucking in charge," Jaden replied. "So hot."

"Yeah?" Ruby said, flicking Jaden's clit.

"Yes," Jaden stated and moved her hands into Ruby's shirt, cupping her breasts.

"Touch me," Ruby requested.

Jaden moved her hands into Ruby's sports bra.

"No, touch me," Ruby said again.

"Oh," Jaden replied, feeling like an idiot.

She moved her hands down to Ruby's shorts, undid them quickly, and moved her hand inside Ruby's underwear, finding her wet.

"God, why do we ever stop having sex?" Jaden asked herself more than Ruby.

Ruby could only laugh in response, and a second later, Jaden's shorts fell to the floor, and Ruby's lips met her own as her fingers moved inside Jaden.

"Oh, yes," Jaden said, stroking Ruby's clit faster now.

"I don't know why we ever stop, either," Ruby said. "When this…" She pushed in deeper. "Feels so good."

Jaden spread her legs wider still, stretching the panties she'd put on that morning, causing Ruby to grunt a little as she thrust inside her.

"By the lake," Jaden said as she continued to stroke Ruby's clit.

"What?" Ruby asked. "I'm so close, babe."

"Tonight, meet me in our… spot. Oh, God." Jaden's body froze in place as her orgasm ripped through her.

She tried to keep up the strokes on Ruby's clit but lost the battle as she could only focus on her own pleasure. A minute later, she realized that Ruby was rubbing against her hand, pressing into Jaden's thigh now. Having recovered from her own orgasm a bit, Jaden slipped inside her, turning them around until Ruby was against the shelves.

"Oh, fuck," Ruby gasped out as Jaden pushed the shorts down for her until they were around her ankles.

"I can tell my dads that I'm staying here to help clean up for the night." Jaden pushed inside deeper. "We can meet... at the lake... and do this... again."

"I'm coming..."

Jaden watched as Ruby came then, loving how she was the cause of the redness on Ruby's neck and cheeks, her mouth in the shape of an O, and her eyes near slits.

"I love you," she said against Ruby's lips. "And I want all summer to be like this."

"Yes," Ruby replied, but Jaden wasn't sure if she was referring to the fact that Jaden was still inside her, helping her come down, or to what she'd just said.

They walked out of the storage closet separately, with Jaden going first. After a trip to the bathroom, Jaden walked outside, planning to run the ring toss booth for her shift, but she bumped into her dads first.

"Hey, sweetie. Having fun?" her dad asked.

"Yeah," she said, putting her hands in her pockets.

She'd washed them, but she wasn't taking any chances.

"Good. This is amazing. We just had our helpline shift, and your dad and I took several calls. I know it's unfortunate that someone would need to call the line, but we both talked to a few young people, and I think we made some good progress."

"That's great," she replied.

"I talked to one of them about coming out, and I think he just might do it."

"Dad, that's awesome," she said.

"Anyway, we're going to enjoy ourselves in the music tent and head home after."

"Okay. I have to stay late and help clean up for tomorrow."

"That's pretty late, honey."

"I know, but Ruby needs the help. I can stay at her place after. Her parents said it would be fine."

"Well, as long as her parents will be there, too."

"They will be. They're helping us clean up and then setting up with us again tomorrow," she said.

While the last part was technically the truth, she hadn't yet asked them if she could stay. Her plan was to meet Ruby by the lake. Ruby would sneak out, and they'd make love by the water. They could sneak into her house after, and Jaden would fall asleep next to her. She'd wake early and go into the guest room before Ruby's parents woke up, and they'd go to day two of the three-day festival together.

"How are things going with you two?" her dad asked.

Jaden felt bad then. She hadn't told her dads much about their relationship or the fact that they'd taken certain steps. She definitely wouldn't tell them about the fact that they'd had sex because her dads would watch her like a hawk all summer if she did that, but she didn't want to not tell them how important Ruby was to her, either.

"We're in love," she replied, smiling. "And we've planned our visits and stuff for the school year."

"In love, huh?" her dad teased her.

"Yes, I love her. She's amazing. She did all this." Jaden motioned around the festival.

"And she makes you happy?"

"So happy," Jaden said, not at all thinking about the storage closet.

"And she treats you well?" her other dad asked.

"Yes, she does."

"Well, that's all we can ask for, isn't it?" her dad said. "We'll let you have fun, okay? Call us tonight once you're at Ruby's so that we know you're safe."

"I will. Love you, guys," she said.

"We love you, too, honey. So much."

Her dads hugged her tightly before walking away.

***

Hours later, Jaden had a blanket in front of the water. Ruby brought them a few flameless candles she'd stolen from her house. They made love under the stars, and when they were finished, Jaden lay against Ruby's naked chest, looking out at the water and the trees beyond as the fireflies lit up the sky.

"Do you think *I* could get into Dexter?" she asked.

"Dexter?" Ruby checked, running a hand through Jaden's hair as her other reached for the blanket on top of them and moved it up a bit to combat the chill.

"Yes, that hard university you got into that is over six hours away from my lame state school."

"You want to go to Dexter?"

"Not this year," Jaden replied. "I need to figure out what I want to do, but I was thinking maybe if I could get in for next year, I could transfer."

"You'd do that?" Ruby asked, sounding excited.

"Maybe. Only if you were there, and you and I were still together." She kissed Ruby's erect nipple. "You're cold. We should go inside."

"I'm not cold," Ruby argued. "I'm turned on."

"Still?" Jaden said, laughing.

"Always around you," Ruby replied. "And I would love it if you ended up at Dexter, but I'd only want you to do that if *you* wanted to."

"Let's see how the fall goes, and maybe I'll apply," Jaden said, moving her lips to Ruby's nipple. "And your parents are home, so if you still need something, you should say so now."

"I need something," Ruby replied, causing Jaden to suck on her nipple in response. "Not that," Ruby told her, laughing. "Look at me, Jade."

Jaden paused and looked up at her.

"I love you," Ruby said.

"I love you, too. What did you need, then?"

"Just to tell you that and to hold you out here a little longer."

"Okay," Jaden replied, smiling at her.

CHAPTER 24

"Someone told me you were the one who started this whole thing," a girl said.

"Sorry?" Ruby replied, looking up from the table she was sitting behind.

"You're the person who started the festival."

"Oh, yeah," Ruby said.

"I just wanted to say thank you."

"To me? Why?" Ruby asked, stacking some brochures for the LGBTQ+ center.

"Well, I called the helpline last night and talked to someone, and it was really helpful, so I'm here today to talk to someone from the center in person," the girl said.

"That's great," Ruby replied, smiling at her.

"You look way too young to be running a festival," the girl noted.

"I had help; it's not like I did the whole thing myself."

"And this is just the first one, right? There will be one every year now?"

Ruby sighed and said, "I hope so. It's a lot of work, and I'm going to college in a few months, so someone else will have to do the bulk of the work. My friend wants to help, so we'll see. The center is interested in a small parade down Main Street at the end of the festival, but that'll take even more work and co-ordination, so... I don't know, honestly. I guess we'll have to figure it out soon."

"I can help. Well, I'm in college, too, but I'm only about an hour away, so I can help whenever."

"You want to help?" Ruby asked.

The girl smiled and said, "I'm going to be a junior, so classes are harder now, but yeah, I want to help. This is something that can help people. It helped me."

Ruby internally sighed in relief. She'd helped someone. She'd maybe made an impact on someone else's life. Maybe even more than just one person.

"I'm glad," Ruby replied.

"I'm not out yet," the girl said.

"Okay."

"But I want to be. I'm going to tell my parents next weekend," she added, smiling. "And there's someone at school that I need to tell as well because I'm completely in love with her, and she has no idea. But I'm ready to shoot my shot." She nodded confidently.

"And this festival helped you with that?"

"Talking to someone who had been there that didn't know me helped, yeah. At school, I'm in a sorority, and I know they'd be supportive, but none of them have come out themselves, so I couldn't really talk to them about it. There's a guy in my lit class that came out last year. He and I are friends now, and we've talked about it. He knows I'm gay. He's the only one who knows, but he knows practically everything about me now, and it's much easier to get an objective opinion from someone who isn't constantly asking me when I'm going to ask the girl I like out on a date."

Ruby swallowed and gave the girl a nod.

"Like I said, I just wanted to say thank you. I've met a lot of people here today already: a few artists and people from the helpline and the center. I think this is amazing. Nothing like this existed where I grew up, and I felt like I was the only one going through things."

"Me too," Ruby shared.

"Not anymore, though," the girl added.

"Not anymore, no," Ruby agreed, smiling.

The girl then walked off without even giving Ruby her name, and Ruby just sat there, looking around the room and wishing she were outside so she could look around the entire festival and finally take it all in. She hadn't done that yet, choosing to focus on the work and making sure everyone was having a good time.

"I'm off-duty," Jaden said, walking up to the table.

"You are?"

"Yes, I was relieved. So I am available in case anyone wants to walk around with me for a while."

"Anyone?" Ruby teased.

"Well, specifically, my amazing girlfriend who has yet to ride a single ride, play a single game, and actually enjoy herself at the thing she built."

Ruby pointed to herself and said, "Me?"

"Yes, you," Jaden laughed. "Come with me, babe."

"I'm here for another hour."

"It's an empty table with a stack of brochures. Plus, my dads are in here somewhere; they'll take care of anyone who walks up." Jaden held out her hand. "I want to have some fun with you."

"We did that last night," Ruby said, standing up.

"And we'll do it again soon, but I didn't mean that."

Ruby laughed and joined Jaden on the other side of the table. She was led outside, and they walked through the packed parking lot until they reached the entrance of the festival. Jaden had been holding her hand, but she let it go to wrap her arm around Ruby from the side and rest her head on her shoulder.

"You did all this," Jaden told her.

"No, I didn't. I called people, and–"

"Ruby, this wouldn't have happened without you. *You* went to the town council. *You* asked your parents to help. *You* gathered volunteers and made those calls. *You've* been here every weekend, nearly every night, and *you've* never stopped. Take it in, babe. People are here standing in tents with rainbow flags hanging from them. People are dressed up. They're buying flags, too. Look – there's the trans flag and the bi flag." Jaden pointed to two people who were wearing flags they'd bought at the festival around their necks like capes. "*You* did all this. And it's wonderful and amazing, and I want you to celebrate it. You are now off-duty for the night. So are Chance and Jo. The four of us are going to have fun, listen to music, eat carnival food, play some games where you'll win me a prize, and ride the rides until we close this place down."

"I can't just shirk my responsibilities," Ruby argued, wrapping an arm around Jaden's shoulders.

"You're not. You have more than enough people here to help. Let's find Chance and Jo. I'm sure they're together. I caught them making out by the cotton candy booth earlier – just out there in the open, full-on making out behind the thing. I was grabbing paper plates to restock the candy apple stand, and Jo had Chance pressed to the back of the damn building. Pretty sure she got to second base."

Ruby laughed and said, "Who would've thought that this summer would start like this? I have a girlfriend; Chance has a girlfriend. We're all celebrating Pride at a festival in my hometown... Crazy."

"Yeah, crazy – crazy perfect. Let's go."

An hour later, Ruby had won Jaden a stuffed bear that she could've bought at a store for cheaper. They'd ridden the Ferris wheel and a few other rides, but the Ferris wheel was Ruby's favorite because they'd made out at the top and, well, all the way around the thing. Then, they'd also shared a funnel cake with strawberries and powdered sugar. When Chance and Jo decided to head over to the main food tent to help clean up before Chance drove Jo home, Ruby decided it was time to ask Jaden a question.

"So... I wanted to check with you about something," she began.

"Okay. What?"

"Well, you know Chance is going to be at her program up until orientation."

"Yeah."

"And we're moving into an apartment..."

"Yes, babe," Jaden said, laughing.

"I've asked my parents if I can go to school myself. I want to do a whole road trip thing. It's only six hours, but I was thinking about maybe stopping in a couple of cool towns along the way and getting there a few days before orientation week so I can get unpacked and settled."

"Okay. Sounds good."

"Jade, will you go with me?"

"On a road trip?"

"Yeah. I was thinking, it would give us a week together before Chance got there. We could stop for a night or two and stay in hotels or just head straight there and have the place to ourselves. I could buy you a plane ticket home so that you have time to pack up and get to school yourself."

"You want to go on a road trip with me?"

"A short one, yeah. I'm ready to be an adult, you know? I just don't want my parents on campus with me, helping me try to find the bookstore or something. I want to figure it out my-self. And they did the whole drop-off thing with my brother, so they said they were cool with it. They'll come on parents' week-end anyway."

"We'd have a full week together where we can do whatever we want before we have to say goodbye?" Jaden asked.

"Yeah," Ruby replied. "And you'd have to help me unpack a little. I've got a bed and some furniture I'll have delivered, so I might need help putting things together, but– "

"Ruby?"

"Yeah?"

"Hell, yes." Jaden laughed. "You and me, a week of just us – I'm there."

"You want to?" Ruby checked.

"Of course, I do." Jaden cupped her cheek. "I love you. I want all the time we can get together."

"I love you, too," Ruby said.

CHAPTER 25

Chance watched as Jo talked to an artist who had some chalk landscapes on display, and Jo seemed to be enjoying herself, laughing and giving the artist a high-five. It was pretty adorable. Chance watched Jo help the artist carry some stuff to a car while Chance packed up the food tent. When Jo looked over and caught Chance staring, Jo smiled back and nodded. Chance followed the nod to the Ferris wheel and nodded back.

It was the last night of the festival. Thankfully, they'd done a lot of packing up already, so they'd be able to get home by one in the morning, and then, they could finally relax. Chance walked to Jo when she finished and couldn't help but think about the fact that she'd be gone in just a couple of weeks. When she took Jo's hand, she tried to push it out of her mind, but by the time they were in the car on the Ferris wheel, Chance was holding on to Jo tightly, not wanting to ever let go.

"Are you okay?" Jo asked her.

"I missed you."

"I missed you, too." Jo held her tightly and kissed the top of Chance's head. "I was wondering if I could tell you something."

Chance looked up and waited.

"I don't know exactly yet," Jo added after a while.

"Don't know what?" Chance asked.

"Just that... I don't know for sure."

"Jo, you're kind of scaring me right now." She tugged on Jo's T-shirt.

"You know how I told you I've never felt like I fit in?"

"Yes."

"And that being gay was only part of it?"

"Yes."

"That's because I've never known that I felt like... It's just when people would call me a girl, it didn't... feel like it was true."

"Oh," Chance said, tilting her head and trying to process.

"I don't feel like a guy, either, though. Like, I don't feel like I'm a different gender; I just don't feel like I fit into either one."

Chance remembered that day at *Carver's* not all that long ago, it felt, where she'd mentioned the word *girl* in reference to Jo, who had turned away then. She thought back on some of their other exchanges and remembered Jo's expressions.

"Have I been saying things that are wrong for you?" she asked as the Ferris wheel car began to move.

"No. I'm still trying to figure things out."

"Okay," Chance replied. "But you'd tell me, right?"

"I was talking to that artist the other day and then again, tonight. They're non-binary, and they referred to me as *they* tonight." Jo smiled softly, staring out at the festival.

"And you liked it?" Chance asked, smiling at Jo.

"Yeah, it's weird. I've started to think of myself that way more and more, too. I'm sure it's hard to understand, but it was like the first time it ever felt right."

"Jo?"

"Yeah?" Jo asked, looking at her now.

"I'm with you, okay?" Chance cupped Jo's cheek. "I'm with you. Whoever you are is… it's who I'm in love with."

Jo's eyes filled with tears, and Chance licked her lips, swallowed, and waited.

"You're in love with me?"

"Yes," Chance confirmed.

"I…"

"You don't have to say it back. I just wanted you to know."

"I'm in love with you," Jo said.

"You *are*?"

Jo nodded and wiped at a tear that had rolled down their cheek.

"Even with what I just told you?" Jo asked. "You're still in love with me?"

"Yes," Chance said, wiping away another of Jo's tears. "What you said doesn't change who you are, Jo. I want you. I want to be with you. I want you to tell me more about who you are and how you want me to refer to you. I just want you to be happy."

"You make me happy," Jo replied, wiping yet another tear. "You make me so happy."

"Okay. Then, we're all good here," Chance concluded, laughing.

"Are you sure? It's a lot, Chance."

"No, it's you. And I'm really happy with you, so I'm good." She leaned in and kissed Jo's cheek.

"Um... Do you maybe want to go to the lake with me tonight?"

"The lake?" Chance asked.

"Yeah, the lake."

"The spot on the lake?" Chance checked.

"If you want."

"What if Ruby and Jaden are there?"

"We can find another spot," Jo offered.

"And we're talking about what *I think* we're talking about, right?" Chance asked.

"If you're ready. If not, we can just be together."

"And you're not..." Chance looked down at her hand that was still wrapped up in Jo's shirt. "It's not just because I'm leaving soon?"

"No," Jo said, taking Chance's hand now. "I've always wanted to have my first time when I was in love with someone."

"Me too," Chance said, swallowing hard. "But we can wait."

"Do you want to?" Jo asked. "We can if you want to."

"I don't even know what to do. I've never even asked Ruby how to–" Chance stopped herself before adding, "I want to make you feel good."

"You do. You will."

"How can you know that?" Chance asked as the wheel continued to move.

"I had my hand in your shirt earlier, and I think I almost... Well, you know."

"You did?"

"I was touching your breast, Chance. Yes, I almost did. I also had my leg between your legs."

"I remember," Chance said, smirking at them. "That felt good."

"It did?" Jo asked.

"Yes." Chance nodded.

"Were you not on your way?" they asked, and even in the darkness, Chance could still see Jo's blush.

"I was," Chance replied. "We were in public, though."

"Behind the stand; no one could see."

"And at the lake later?" Chance asked.

"Yeah?" Jo asked, leaning in.

"We would technically be in public."

"Right. Not tonight, then. We can just hold each other. My mom knows I'll be here late, so we would have at least a couple of hours before she'd expect you to drop me off."

"What if we just go to the lake to hold each other but see how it goes? If it happens, it happens. If it doesn't, it will another time."

Jo nodded slowly, leaned in, and kissed her.

***

Two hours later, they were sitting at the lake on a blanket Chance had in her trunk. Jo was sitting right next to her, twisting a blade of grass around just to have something to do with her hands. Chance watched as Jo stared out at the water and realized she'd just used the female pronouns to refer to Jo in her mind. It would require some practice for her to make sure to always use the right ones for Jo, but she didn't mind at all.

Staring at Jo all night tonight, Chance had seen a change in Jo. They seemed to be more confident now, more comfortable in their skin. It was a beautiful thing to see, and it was also a turn-on.

"Jo?"

"Yeah?" Jo looked at her.

Chance lay down on the blanket and reached for the button on her khaki shorts. Jo's eyes followed and went wide as Chance undid the button and then the zipper. Jo tossed the blade of grass somewhere on the pebbles and licked their lips. Then, they reached for the hem of their shirt, looking at Chance, asking silent permission. Chance nodded, and the shirt was gone. Jo was left in a sports bra and their jean shorts. Then, Jo moved until they were on top of Chance, and Chance looked up at them and smiled.

"I love you," she said softly. "I'm ready."

Jo nodded and said, "I can't believe I'm this lucky. I saw you that day at the first meeting, and I just knew, Chance. I knew, but I never thought we'd end up here."

"We're not ending up here," Chance said, taking Jo's hand and moving it under her own shirt, up to her breast. "We're just getting started."

EPILOGUE

To Whom It May Concern,

If you're reading this, someone handed you this at the festival or the parade, and you're probably wondering why we've written you a letter. Well, several years ago, we held the very first Pride festival in our tiny town. It was a major group effort, but four of us worked hard to make it happen, and now it's happening every year, which is pretty amazing. Ruby started this with an idea, and Chance was the one who was there from the beginning to support her. Jaden and Jo joined at that first meeting, and things started to move.

Why should you care? Well, the festival grew, and now it's a parade down Main Street in celebration of love being love and people being whoever they were born to be. It's the fourth year of the festival and the third year for the parade. Thousands of people turn up each year now. We have a fully staffed helpline 24/7, lots of local artists who are able to sell their work regularly, more volunteers for the LGBTQ+ center, and more acceptance and understanding.

This year, we decided to write letters to anyone who might need to hear this. If this has been handed to you, it's because you've spoken with a volunteer who recognized you might need to know something – it gets better.

Yeah, we know; that's a cliché now. But it's the truth, too. It does get better. If you feel alone, talk to someone here. If you're wondering if you're the only one who's ever gone through this, you're not. Your journey is your own, but we're happy to help however we can.

Our lives were made infinitely better when we each accepted who we were and when we went for what we wanted, and we want and hope for the same for you and for everyone else. At the bottom of this letter, we've listed helpful resources in case you need them. We want you to know that you matter; your story, your life, who you're meant to become – it all matters. And people here will help you however we can. So, remember that, and reach out when you need to.

Sincerely,
Ruby, Chance, Jaden, and Jo
Original Festival Organizers

Jo and Jaden hadn't thought they should be listed as organizers since it had really been more Ruby and Chance, but Ruby and Chance had insisted. And now, there were these letters that got handed around to anyone who needed them, and they'd do it again the next year and the year after that as well.

Ruby and Chance were about to graduate from college. Jaden still had one semester to go since she'd transferred to Dexter her sophomore year, and some of her classes didn't count there. Ruby would be remaining in the apartment they now shared and would take a few classes just for fun and because she could while Jaden finished up. Ruby also had a campus job and had resumes out to companies near Dexter, which was where Jaden and she wanted to settle down. Well, settle for a while, at least. They weren't sure they wanted to spend their whole lives there, but for now, they had an apartment, jobs, and school, so it worked for them.

Jo had gotten into school about two hours south of Dexter, and thanks to their scholarship, they'd been able to live in the dorms. They still had a year left, and now that Chance was finished with school, she'd join Jo, and they'd rent an apartment together for the first time for Jo's senior year. Chance had already lined up an entry-level job about thirty minutes away.

The festival had continued in large part because of Jo's determination to make it happen even with everyone else moving away. Jo had partnered with organizations, got the town council to see the benefits of making it an annual tradition, and once they'd graduated, they'd handed it off to someone else.

Now, they were all sitting by the lake after a long day of volunteering at various games and booths.

Jaden was sitting between Ruby's legs, drawing circles on Ruby's knee with her fingertip. Jo was lying with their head in Chance's lap as Chance ran her fingers through Jo's still messy hair.

"So, tomorrow is the parade," Ruby said.

"Yeah," Chance echoed, looking down at Jo, who had their eyes closed.

"Crazy, huh? I feel like it just happened."

"Yeah," Jaden replied, sounding tired. "Can we maybe get to bed, babe? We have an early day tomorrow."

"Us, too?" Jo asked Chance.

"I'm okay if you want to just fall asleep on me right here," Chance replied, winking down at Jo.

"Chance…"

Chance met Ruby's eyes and understood instantly that Ruby wanted them to go.

"Um… Actually, yeah. Let's go."

"Yeah?" Jo asked. "My mom's place? She's staying with her boyfriend tonight."

"Whole house to ourselves? I'm in."

They stood slowly, feeling their muscles ache as they stretched. Chance looked at Ruby again, who gave her the expression that told her it was about to happen.

"Come on, hot stuff," Chance encouraged. "Let's take advantage of being alone in the house."

Chance and Jo walked toward Chance's car that was parked in Ruby's driveway.

"It's happening, isn't it?" Jo asked her.

"I think so," Chance replied. "Think Jaden will say yes?"

"I can't imagine she's going to say no – she's got bridal magazines at their apartment."

Chance laughed and said, "I think Ruby took the hint."

"They're only twenty-two," Jo remarked, climbing into the passenger seat.

"They're not getting married *now*," Chance replied, climbing in next to them. "They just want to take this step. I can't see them having a wedding for another three or four years, at least.

Ruby wants to get her career going, and I think Jaden does, too. They just know this is what they want."

"I know what *I* want," Jo stated.

Chance turned to them and said, "You do?"

"Yes." Jo nodded. "You. Me. Forever."

"I want that, too," Chance replied.

"So, do you need the ring right now?"

"No," Chance said, laughing. "I don't need a ring at all. Just need you, Jo."

Jo smiled over at her and then said seriously, "I'll get you a damn ring one day, Chance. I want people to know you have someone."

"Then, just get me the ring; we don't have to do the whole engagement/marriage thing just because everyone else wants to. You get me a ring, and I'll wear it. I'll get you one, too, if you want it. The only thing I care about is that you and I are to-gether."

"I love you," Jo replied, shaking their head. "How are you *this* cool?"

Chance laughed and said, "Let's just go to your mom's place, and you can figure out how you can thank me for being so cool maybe two times before Ruby calls us to tell us that Jaden said yes."

"*Three* times," Jo said. "They're going to have sex out there for a while before they come up for air."

Chance laughed and said, "Hey, Jo?"

"Yeah?" Jo took Chance's hand.

"What we said in that letter thing we all wrote…"

"What about it?" Jo asked.

"Our lives are infinitely better because of that festival."

Jo smiled at her and said, "Yeah, they are."

AFTERWORD

Celebrate love with the I Heart SapphFic Pride Collection, eight stand-alone romances offering a taste of the very best modern sapphic fiction has to offer.

Be sure to subscribe to I Heart SapphFic to discover the latest in sapphic fiction every week! Because love is love, and everyone deserves a happily ever after.

IHeartSapphFic.com

www.ingramcontent.com/pod-product-compliance
Lightning Source LLC
Chambersburg PA
CBHW030345180626
46812CB00007B/2769